No-one Died

ZAK RUSS

Honeybee Books

Published by Honeybee Books
Broadoak, Dorset
www.honeybeebooks.co.uk

Printed in the UK using paper from sustainable sources

ISBN: 978-1-910616-97-0

World Birth and Death Rates

Birth Rate	Death Rate
• 19 births/1,000 population	• 8 deaths/1,000 population
• 131.4 million births per year	• 55.3 million people die each year
• 360,000 births per day	• 151,600 people die each day
• 15,000 births each hour	• 6,316 people die each hour

'Mortality rates have decreased across all age groups worldwide during the last 5 decades, and deaths in children younger than 5 years decreased to less than 5 million for the first time. However, these decreases are not uniform, and there remains significant diversity in certain components of age-specific mortality in some countries.'

'These are among the findings recently published in the Lancet in a series of studies that make up the Global Burden of Disease Study 2016. More than 2,500 researchers from more than 130 countries and territories covering a broad spectrum of specialties examined 330 injuries, diseases and causes of death in 195 countries and territories during varying periods of time from 1970 to 2016.'

Book 1

Global Tragedy

"Here's the bottom line. Patients can beat this disease. And we can beat this disease. But we have to stay vigilant. We have to work together at every level — federal, state and local. And we have to keep leading the global response, because the best way to stop this disease, the best way to keep Americans safe, is to stop it at its source — in West Africa."

President Obama, October 25, 2014

The World as it is. 31 December 2021:

London, just another death.

The Accident and Emergency Department of The Royal London Hospital on Whitechapel Road was surprisingly quiet for a New Years Eve. As the clock counted down the minutes and seconds to the expected chimes of the newly re-installed Big Ben, the on duty crews in the 'Resus' cubicles had time to take stock on their busy year and reflect on what 2022 may bring. A rare moment of reflection before the usual influx of New Year revellers, attempted suicides and those unfortunate enough to fall sick during the annual celebrations accompanying this point of the Earth's natural progression on its orbit around the Sun.

On-duty Doctor Anatoly Romanov, called Tony by his friends and colleagues, unusually had time to collect his thoughts and contemplate the tragedies that had engulfed the world in the past year. 2021, what a year this had been for health services around the world! The huge Ebola outbreak in Central Africa, its spread to Eastern Europe, the Middle East and the Indian sub-continent, followed by the emergence of the same strain of Ebola in the USA, with a resultant huge toll of human life on the American Continent. In a time when life expectancy was generally better, at least in the Western world, there had been a series of calamitous outbreaks of disease with huge death tolls; 20 million in Europe, 30 million in the Americas, uncountable millions in India, Africa and the Middle East. All followed by huge international efforts to develop vaccines and medications to deal with each of these catastrophes. All at a cost to those stricken, of course, nothing is free in this world driven by business bottom line and share price.

From the point of view of the UK's still just functioning National Health Service, they had got off lightly. Ironically, the UK was protected by a self-imposed isolation due to the still on-going political crisis over Brexit, resulting in fewer immigrants wishing to enter a mostly unwelcoming country. Once effective medications had been created and made available, they had been delivered to the largely unaffected UK population quickly and efficiently. No great loss of life, no great panic, even though just over the channel people had been dying in their thousands. It was also regarded as serendipity that the usually sub-standard IT systems of the NHS had been up-graded with stuff that actually worked and was fit for purpose, just before the time they would actually be needed to manage the huge, nation-wide anti-Ebola vaccination programme. Unusually, the Wi-Fi worked throughout the hospital premises. Maybe this time the systems would continue to work and would not prove difficult to use, driving doctors, nurses and administrators to suicidal levels of anxiety because the 'computer says no'. Even more unusual the whole lot had come from a single supplier, a Chinese company, in a single project for the whole of the UK NHS. Strangely no hospital management staff admitted to knowing that this project was underway. An odd development really, when you took into account the political uproar of previous years, when Chinese companies had been contracted for providing the backbone for National Communications Networks. He'd thought at the time that the furore over use of Huawei was utter nonsense. If it works reliably, is fit for the purpose intended and fits the price, use it. He looked up at the nearest IT hub, neatly positioned in the corner of the A&E ward. What was the name embossed on the casing?

Looked like Zhang or something. He'd not heard of the company, but, you know what, everything seemed to work much better than before. The installation of the new systems had also been remarkably efficient. The teams had been into the hospital at the end of August, installed all that needed to be in place and had left within the week. As usual though, training in use of the systems lagged behind and it had not been until just before the vaccines arrived that training for the staff had been completed. Everything was done the modern way; just in time. One outstanding feature in all of this was the new helpdesk system. Allegedly reaching all the way back to the Chinese system providers, there was always somebody there, and without fail they solved any IT issue quickly.

So, surely this was a great portent for 2022. This year had to be better, with even more funding being promised by the new UK Unity Government elected only 30 days ago after the final failure of the last iteration of the embattled Tory Government. Tony was of Russian origin, but had chosen to live and work in the UK. He was not into politics, preferring to keep his mind focussed on medical issues, but, like almost everyone else he was relieved when the old UK systems of political parties and first past the post voting had finally been proved unfit for purpose in the 21st century. The new UK Unity Government seemed to have pulled in all the best political minds and had been formed within a new system of proportional representation. The result so far seemed to be that things were actually getting done. Of course, there were always those who yearned for the past and bemoaned their own loss of influence, but, from what he could see, the UK public was beginning to unite around this more collaborative, not combative, Parliament.

Tony reflected that the National Health Service had managed to remain intact and keep delivering medical care when needed, despite failed promises, and continuous attempts by the previous government to sell off the assets to US health-care providers. Some even postulated that this would be the price of receiving the new Ebola vaccines. A narrow escape, but the new Unity Government looked set to review and renew the whole direction of the UK, and, importantly, to prioritise much needed assistance to the NHS. Well, that's what the politicians were saying anyway.

Tony took advantage of this unexpected quiet period to check in on one of his longer term patients. The lady, who had been a long time neighbour of Tony in North London, was in a bad way. Admitted onto the ward 15 days ago, Brooklyn Walters, had a previously undiagnosed tumour attached to her liver and bowel, and it had proved inoperable. Brooklyn was not expected to see out many more hours on this earth. He headed upstairs to the ward at 1155pm, and as he approached, the seconds ticking past 1159pm, he noticed the nurse, ward sister and ward doctor around her bed. Tony knew Brooklyn had a Do Not Attempt Resuscitation Order in place, so no attempt would be made to bring her back when the inevitable worst happened. As he approached the bed, he heard the chimes of Big Ben from some radio on the ward, and the ward doctor, Peter Talon, calmly announcing time of death as the last chime rang out.

Brooklyn Walters, librarian, 50 years old, no age at all, lived all her life in London, the last person to die of natural causes in the UK in 2021; Time of Death 23:59:59 GMT.

The World as it is. 31 December 2021.

Damascus, just another day in paradise.

The final days of 2021 for Dr Butrus Azrak arrived in a somewhat different style. No rest here, plenty of inward reflection on the civil war still raging after so many years, but no rest. Of necessity the fighting had stopped for several months in the middle of the year, due to the outbreak of an especially malignant variant of Ebola, which had emerged from Africa, swept through the Middle East, India, and Asia and eventually into Eastern Europe.

He remembered the panic as the death toll rose and the disease began to spread into other, more prosperous regions. The fear of the disease moving into the Western World kicked off the mad rush to develop vaccines, a cure, something. These had eventually emerged from various research establishments in the USA and China. Some said, with such haste that correct testing procedures could not have been followed, but a solution was needed now, not after the world had been denuded of human beings. The World Health Organisation had then coerced, even forced, the USA and China to work together, to get these badly needed medicines to affected areas. In the case of Syria this involved lifting sanctions imposed by the USA on the barely surviving Assad regime, to allow lives to be saved. The vaccines that had been distributed, not enough for all it seemed, had worked. Many lives saved. Many lives were also lost. The available records showed that there were no survivors, among those not lucky enough to be chosen for the vaccination programme. Butrus reflected on the heartbreak of this whole vaccination process. He had known nothing like it in the past. Only those on the government list, and who could physically be brought into the hospitals were vaccinated. Most mystifying of all was the fact that vaccination teams were not allowed out into the wider Syria area at all. The special security detachments of the Syrian, and occasionally Russian military, made sure that rules were not broken by hospital staff. They also oversaw the roll out of the new IT equipment, installed in hospitals to assist in management of the vaccination programme. This included new mobile phone masts erected around the whole district, placed in secured compounds and ensuring for the first time ever, to Butrus's knowledge, that he had been able to get a usable mobile phone, and even 5G, signal. No vaccinations occurred until the full IT system refits were complete, the military security teams saw to that. No explanations were given for this, just orders from the very highest. The most bizarre thing about this was that, as part of the vaccination, people had to have a special microchip inserted on top of the left hand. The explanation for this in the official orders was that progress of the vaccination needed to be checked with a special reader supplied with the new IT systems and any reactions to the vaccination needed to be reported immediately. Butrus had no idea where the money came from for all of this, or why you would need each individual to be chipped, like a pet animal, just to check progress of a vaccination. He did not question, he was just thankful the vaccination programme seemed to be working, and grateful to the Chinese provider of all this wonderful new IT, Zhang Medical Systems.

Now, here in Damascus, as the year of 2021 neared its end, the civil war had been re-ignited by those lucky enough to have been vaccinated and survive the disease. You would think nobody would have the energy or inclination for more fighting wouldn't you? Butrus did not follow politics, and indeed up until the outbreak he had thought of politicians as being the severest threat to humanity. He was not into the warfare they caused; he just tried to fix the broken bodies caused by this pointless conflict. He hoped for better in 2022, but suspected things would remain the same, or maybe get worse, for a long time yet.

The doorbell for the ward rang. Butrus looked towards the door and saw the familiar face of Sister Beth from the Salesian Sisters Hospital in Damascus. Sister Beth was a very capable nurse. First and foremost, though, a nun who saw herself in the service of God, delivering medical help to the poorest in Damascus, notwithstanding political or religious belief. Butrus admired her immensely. She and her small team of nuns had ensured that the Salesian Sisters Hospital, funded by the Vatican and a host of other charities, had been able to get the new vaccinations against Ebola directly to many of the poorest Syrians in the district, even those whose names could not be found on any government list. He knew he himself had worked hard to try to do this, but in the end, it had seemed that the vaccination list for the Damascus Hospital comprised only the establishment, those deemed worthy, and those who could pay. Sister Beth was without doubt a force of nature, backed fully by Vatican resources.

Butrus moved to the door, opened the lock and let in Sister Beth. Behind her were two of the other nuns, Sister Mary and Sister Faye, pushing a hospital trolley with what looked like just a large pile of rags on top. He noticed the mark on the back of Sister Beth's left hand where the vaccination chip had been inserted. Beth had actually had a crucifix tattoo over the site of the chip. The other two Sisters had the same tattoo. Vatican orders no doubt.

Sister Beth turned around and dragged the trolley though

the open door. 'Can you help us Butrus? This is Brother Dominic from our outreach centre near Aleppo. He was taken ill a couple of days ago and made his way back to us, but just collapsed tonight and we have no beds free.'

Butrus nodded. 'Bring him in and let's see what is happening.'

'Looking at him, I'm pretty sure it's a stroke, and a bad one, but we have no method of helping him at our hospital.' said Beth.

'We will have to look at him here in the corridor, Sister Beth. As you can see all our treatment booths are full at the moment.' He called over a nurse to assist him, and began the primary survey work.

Sister Beth looked around. Butrus was right. In the first booth was a young man, his right leg off at the knee, sedated but still grimacing with pain. The next one along, contained a young woman giving birth. Then a young boy with a bloody laceration on his forehead and his right arm swathed in bandages, crying pitifully. Sister Beth had not noticed the constant chatter of the care teams working when she entered with her patient, but it was evident now as she focussed on the booths. Accident and Emergency Departments were the same the world over; pain, misery, fear of death with ordinary people doing extraordinary work to save them.

Sister Beth turned back to Butrus and watched as he skilfully assessed Brother Dominic. Suddenly Butrus shouted out, 'He's in cardiac arrest, get the defibrillator now'.

The Nurse ran off to grab the machine, as Butrus ripped open Brother Dominic's clothing immediately starting CPR on the exposed chest. Butrus could feel the ribs cracking as he forcefully pumped the heart to keep blood flowing around Brother Dominic's vital organs. No time to worry about the ribs, at this point Brother Dominic was dead anyway. The Nurse arrived back with the defibrillator and rapidly extracted it from the case. The defibrillator began to shout out its instructions, but Butrus and the Nurse didn't need them. They automatically extracted the electronic pads, attached them to Brother Dominic and waited for the analysis to come back. Shock now, said the machine.

Butrus ordered, 'Stand clear. Shocking!' He pushed the button and Brother Dominic's body jerked on the trolley.

'Continue CPR' intoned the defibrillator machine. Butrus was immediately back on the chest delivering CPR, until the defibrillator called a halt to enable analysis. Another shock requested, followed by more CPR, then another shock, more CPR, one more shock. No response.

Butrus checked for vital signs on Brother Dominic. No pulse. He checked for breathing. Nothing: no life signs.

He turned to Sister Beth. 'I'm sorry Beth, I'm afraid Brother Dominic is past our help.'

He addressed the Nurse, and as he spoke he could hear the crackling of loud fireworks outside; 'Time of Death 23:59, very nearly midnight.' As he carefully placed Brother Dominic's hands over his chest Butrus noticed he did not have the tattoo on his left hand. He wondered if he had given his vaccination to some other poor unfortunate Syrian. He imagined that he probably had.

Brother Dominic Anders, Monk from Copenhagen, serving God by helping people of all faiths in Syria: The last person to die of natural causes in Syria; 23:59:59, Local Syrian Time, 31 December 2021.

The World as it was. 2021.

A Fatal Year

How did this whole thing start? Difficult to tell, but terrible, almost unimaginable, stories of large scale death had begun to emerge from the African continent at the beginning of the year.

The nightmare scenario of all nightmare scenarios had slowly crept out of the dark jungles of Africa. A nightmare scenario even for a vast continent used to nightmare scenarios on gigantic scales. A particularly virulent strain of Ebola, seemingly resistant to any known, or imagined, treatments had erupted throughout West and Central Africa. Experts began to notice, then study the rapid spread of the outbreak, and then eventually put forward a hypothesis that this strain had spread much further and much quicker than normal Ebola due to an unexpected migration of fruit bats. Fruit bats? It had been thought for some time that fruit bats could be natural Ebola virus hosts, and this was borne out by the mystifying mass migration flight of fruit bats through Central Africa, which left an ever increasing thick carpet of Ebola victims in its wake. Even more mystifying was the absolute resistance of this strain to known vaccines and treatments. Vaccine stocks were used up, and the death toll still rose.

Why were the bats migrating, why were they carrying this new strain of Ebola, how had this new strain developed? These were the questions experts and heads of governments were struggling with, while medical staff and aid workers on the ground died along with their patients. Nobody seemed able to come up with any smart answers or credible theories.

Who would really care though? This was in Africa, a long way from many supposedly more advanced societies and nations, and this sort of thing happened all the time in Africa, did it not? The usual charities and international aid agencies kept on ringing the alarm bells about this particular outbreak, as the fruit bats continued their seemingly endless migrational flights around Africa, the outbreak spread and many more people died agonising deaths. Grotesque images of people dying appeared on TV screens, were posted on countless social media platforms and discussed in many video calls between friends, professional colleagues and international action groups. The twittersphere buzzed with new stories, each one scarier than the last. Could this all be true, or was it just all fake news? People responded to charitable appeals in the usual way, throwing a few dollars, pounds or Euros into the many collecting tins or donating on-line to the numerous small charitable groups determined to make every effort to improve the lives of ordinary folks in poverty stricken areas world-wide.

Pick your charity, pay your money, consciences salved, the issue quickly forgotten or conveniently filed as just another health crisis for Africa, for somebody else to solve.

Aid workers and health workers made the best of what they had, but in the end became overwhelmed by the sheer scale of death and suffering caused by the outbreak. Volunteers died alongside the people they were volunteering to help. For a while, it all became just the normal news from Africa, but, you know, what did it matter? The USA and China were still following their trade war tit-for-tat tariff hikes, the Middle East was still in conflict centred on Syria, Russia and the EU were still arguing about responsibility for the latest round of cyber-attacks and in London the FTSE continued to slide. These things were more important, right?

Then it all changed. The 1989 Reston, Virginia, scenario re-emerged in the USA at the beginning of March 2021. The public had mostly forgotten about this outbreak caused by a shipment of cynomolgous monkeys transported from the Philippine Islands to Reston, Virginia in 1989. The big difference in this outbreak was, instead of infected primates dying from the Ebola virus, it was human beings, and on a much greater scale. Infected individuals travelling out of Africa and into the USA via sea and air began dying on US soil, and it became clear that the Ebola strain had mutated sufficiently to spread easily from human being to human being with no need for interim animal hosts. Worse still, the vaccines and protocols developed to protect the public from Ebola-Reston, medically known as REBOV/RESTV, did not work. The same began happening in China as Chinese nationals returned home from contract work in parts of Africa. The arrival of infected illegal immigrants began the same process with the populations of southern Europe. The world press began to pull together stories from different parts of the globe and panic spread. Death tolls rose in western countries and governments quickly learned to become interested, as public alarm escalated. No state of emergency address was ever given in the USA, but it was obvious that things were advancing rapidly, and something needed to be done to prevent a global catastrophe. There was no way to denounce this as fake news.

The USA and China halted their extended trade war, some say under pressure from the World Health Organisation, and both countries jointly funded emergency research to find a workable vaccine. Other more affluent regions, clearly seeing the approaching human catastrophe, contributed to the overall effort and re-focussed their medical researchers onto the problem. It was the Chinese researchers and scientists who came up with the goods first, some would say in an unfeasibly short space of time. Vaccine doses were produced and China struck a deal with the USA to distribute the vaccine globally and end all tariff wars between the USA and China. It could be said, commercial realpolitik had won the day. Experts complained that the vaccine had not had time to be properly tested, quoting endless testing regimes and protocols that had not been followed. The USA and China produced their own experts to state categorically that everything had been developed and tested according to the Federal Food and Drug Administration (FDA) agreed process, albeit in a much more speedy fashion, which reflected the dire situation threatening to engulf the human inhabitants of the world as a whole. No time for processes that slowed things up. Humanity was on a fast-track to extinction and corners needed to be cut.

In the terminology of the sitting President of the USA, as he gave one of his ever more rare press conferences: 'We can spend more time testing, but, hey guys, we have a solution, it works and we are saving the world here. These Chinese are good guys, I trust them, and they have come up with the answer. We are beginning to manufacture and distribute the vaccines now. Congress, Senate and I, the President of the USA, are as one on this. Whatever it takes, we will stop this deadly disease. We will do our jobs and protect Americans.'

No more questions were taken by POTUS. He exited the White House conference room and, simultaneously, shares in pharmaceutical companies went through the roof. Many questioned the President's focus on protecting Americans, but his hard-line supporters loved him all the more for it. More forward looking American citizens hated it, and within a couple of weeks this President was gone, impeached for underhand trading deals on medical stocks, and replaced by a more global focussed President and administration. No matter, the trading floors in the USA and China had a series of great surges, made even more sustainable with the advent of the new, more capable administration.

The new President, and Chinese government colleagues, briefed world leaders on the proposed vaccination program and vaccines began being distributed towards the end of September 2021. National Governments were in no position to negotiate on the price as they purchased the many million doses needed to protect their populations, or at least those deemed worthy of protecting; Supply and demand, right? It's just business.

To many, the business simply was life or death. Nobody complained to their governments about the cost of the vaccines. Pay the money or die; that was the only consideration. By a gargantuan effort of logistics, places that had recognised populations that could be counted received vaccines. All of these vaccinations had been used by the end of November 2021. Anybody not vaccinated by then was dead or about to die. The real field test of the vaccine had begun. Wall Street celebrated.

End of crisis, back to the real world, for now.

The Solution. March 2021.

The Dragon rises.

Since the publication of China's first public health plan, back in 2016, the growth in medical research in China had been phenomenal. The existing 32 national centres of clinical research had grown to over 100 by the time of the initial outbreaks of virulent strain Ebola at the end of 2020. This growth had been driven by the Chinese government broadening its national development agenda away from purely economic development and into other areas of national development, including a strong focus on improving the nation's health. Improving the general level of health in a country the size of China though, is not a trivial task. Vast geography, population complexities, wide demographics, huge divides between rich and poor, all added to the task, but, guess what, also gave unimagined opportunities for the new research centres to study complex problems of rare diseases, disease management and health system design. Chinese economic growth and increased investment in science thrust China into a revolution in medical research.

Of course, it goes without saying, the Chinese Government, as pragmatic in its approach to healthcare development, as in all sectors of the economy, began to play all its aces. It had been known, or at least suspected by many other national governments that the Chinese State Cyber-Warfare capability was ultra advanced, and capable of conducting long term cyber incursions into just about anybody's networks. New Chinese medical research facilities needed to get up and running quickly, so the state turned its attention on acquiring 'facts'; in fact, as much medical research data from as many sources as possible. Data, data, data, that was the call from the government to its electronic spies. It must be said the State Cyber-Warfare teams responded magnificently and collected, collected, collected. The slender electronic fingers stretched and reached into the very depths of systems, focussing on universities, medical research facilities, and supposedly secret government departments globally. The stolen data meandered its way into multiple big data computer systems, specifically built in secretive data farms. All of this funded, driven and secured, directly from governmental coffers. About as secretive as you can be in this digital age, and all developed in an astonishingly short space of time.

This government focus kick-started a pace of development simply not possible in Western democracies, increasingly driven by fiscal policies demanding financial retrenchment, not imaginative development. Add to that intransigent, divided governments constantly demanding ever greater oversight of spending, and the potential for decline accelerated. So, China had the chance to create a global monopoly in medical research and it did.

This is why, one early Spring day in 2021, an unattributed piece of research landed on the desk of Doctor Zhang Jin. It did actually land on his desk, in a non-descript brown folder, flying directly from the hand of the Head of the Beijing Medical Research Centre, Professor Wang Hu.

'Dr Zhang, your English is excellent. Take a look at this. I want a full assessment by four o'clock this afternoon. You know what we are looking for.' Wang Hu then headed off in the direction of Laboratory Number 1.

Zhang Jin took a little time to reflect on the famous lack of management soft skills possessed by Wang Hu, but only a little time. After all it was well known around the Institute that as a mentor, a boss and a fellow scientist, Wang Hu was the best. Time was the critical factor here and the hunt was on to find a cure for the Ebola strain currently threatening to kill off humanity in its entirety. Zhang Jin knew English well, because he had been fortunate enough to study at Cambridge University. He opened the folder and examined the contents. He had long ago learned that he was not to question where the information he received came from, but a cursory look at the initial report told him that he was dealing with American English not English English. To be fair, Wang Hu spoke English at least as good as Zhang Jin, so he guessed he had already made a preliminary assessment that there may be something useful in this information.

He looked at the title; Nanobots in targeted applications in the Human Body.

Yes, this was something he recalled being studied in the USA at various institutes and also by a good friend of his in the Chinese University of Hong Kong. There were potential uses for nanobots in medicine. He tried to recall the problems which were associated with this stream of research and he remembered that maybe the control of nanobots inside the human body had been an issue. Nobody wanted renegade nanobots rampaging around their organs, or heaven forbid, replicating and causing more issues. He delved a little further into the documentation and found what he was looking for. No field testing, but controlled laboratory testing, specifically targeting swarms of nanobots against cancerous cell samples. Partially successful, but precise control was the issue. He also recalled some previous information, coming from where, as usual, he did not know, concerning experimental work controlling swarms of nanobots with localised magnetic fields. Essentially, using magnetic fields to drive nanobots in swarms to parts of the body where they could deliver life saving treatments. Looked interesting!

Zhang Jin was intrigued by the possibilities that opened up in terms of the current crisis. He picked up the desk-phone and dialled Wang Hu's number. No mobile phones allowed in this part of the Institute, security orders. Wang Hu picked up the phone.

'Hello.' he said, a man of few words it would seem.

'Professor, its Zhang Jin here. I need to go much deeper into this piece of research. We may have something to base a theory on. It would help greatly if I could have direct access to the Data Centre. It is possible we may have more information to help with this, hidden away in other research topics, and I need to extract it quickly. Can I have authority to deal direct with the Data Centre?'

Wang Hu stayed silent for a few moments.

'It is important Professor, we may be able to leverage some existing tested theories to push forward some solutions to our problem pretty quickly.' Zhang Jin added.

Wang Hu sighed heavily and spoke. 'You know, Zhang Jin, how difficult it is to allow direct contact with Data Centre operations. You know the security hoops we have to jump through. Do you think we have sufficient grounds to believe we may be able to propose workable solutions based on this research?'

Zhang Jin thought hard for a moment. 'It looks like there has been significant advance in the nanobot theory, and we have some complementary activity on control of nanobots that we may be able to combine. I think this may offer the best opportunity yet, and I need to have access to any other data we may have, from whatever source. We need to try.'

Wang Hu responded. 'OK, I will try and get you the access. I still want an initial brief in my office at 4pm.' He put the phone down.

Zhang Jin replaced his handset and returned his attention to the report, and began to put together his thoughts for the 4pm meeting.

The Solution. April 2021:

TechnoMed?

Wang Hu was tired. He removed his round spectacles and rubbed his eyes. At this point he was feeling all of his 65 years. He cleaned the lenses, placed his spectacles slowly and carefully back on the bridge of his nose and, pushing way a few untidy hairs, hooked the frames behind his ears. He raised his head slightly and looked back at the large screen on his office wall. Zhang Jin was stood beside the screen, looking very relieved that he had come to the end of his presentation. Wang Hu carefully studied the faces of Zhang Jin and his small team of researchers. A small team yes, security had insisted on this, but each one bringing exceptional skills to the resolution of this particular problem. Wang Hu was tired, tired from the continuous pressure of pushing the government to understand the need to keep on allocating more and more expensive resource to this project. He was convinced that Zhang Jin and his team had come up with the answer, and he felt pleased that he had personally selected Zhang Jin to lead the project.

Now would come the difficult part. It would require more than just the resources of China to deploy this type of vaccine. He would need to go back to the government and propose that a joint China-USA solution was put to the world; after all, even though nobody wanted to admit it, the basis for this innovative approach had been electronically stolen from USA research facilities. Well, they did not appear to be developing this, so why not China! He supposed that the argument would not be that simple. Anyway, before the next hurdle, one more check of the facts.

'Zhang Jin, you know we have thrown every possible resource into this problem. There is no government official we have not convinced to support us. The investment required will be astronomical, the returns also, if we were thinking in terms of capitalism and not just preventing the human race being wiped off the face of the Earth. We need to be 100% sure now.' Wang Hu looked intently at Zhang Jin and his team. 'Tell me again the main points. Firstly, about the nanobots themselves, and secondly, the critical points of their control'.

Zhang Jin took a deep breath and began once again. 'As you know, we followed up in more depth on the initial piece of research, speculating that nanobots, microscopic particle, can be constructed and then focused onto specific cells in the human body. We tied this into further research from other areas which has already been making progress using nanobots to destroy cancerous cells. All very theoretical with some experimentation completed. We have replicated some of the experimentation, and also looked at the major problem of introducing nanonbots into the human body.'

'The control of nanobots, yes?' interjected Wang Hu. 'Tell me again, how do you ensure the nanobots only attack the cells and viruses that you want them to attack, and stop them rampaging through all cells in the body?'

'You are correct to highlight this aspect, Professor. As you know, this is where other research establishments have hit problems, but that is only one of the challenges. For the control issue, some have looked at using magnetic fields to attract swarms of nanobots onto target cells. This looked promising, but we felt not as accurate or dependable as we would like.

So, we have taken this a stage further. We don't want to have swarms of nanobots, we want to have nanobot teams that work as sensors or destroyers of target cells. Essentially, we have developed a system of hunter-killer teams. Our chosen method is to grow our nanobots organically around a microscopic semi-conductor and metal base, with an exterior coating to prevent the body's immune system from destroying the nanobots. To allow the nanobots to be injected into the human body and not cause obstructions, we have calculated that each nanobot can only be of the size 0.5 to 3 microns. We have experimented on making a standard size of 0.9 micron nanobot, and we believe this to be the optimum size for the use it is designed for.' At this point Zhang Jin stopped speaking, to allow the complexities to sink in.

Wang Hu broke the silence to offer his own understanding. 'So, the choice of this size is to ensure we do not block capillary flow. Anything above 3 microns is likely to do this.'

'Correct, the smaller we can make these nanobots the better.' responded Zhang Jin. 'And the good news for us is that here in China we already have the facilities to produce these nanobots, thanks to our huge computer recycling and micro-electronics enterprises. Our recycling plants can extract many of the materials we need to construct the nanobots, and our micro-electronics producers can be re-tasked, we just need governmental direction to begin the process.'

Zhang paused, gathering his thoughts before continuing. 'The nanobot hunter-killer teams will be programmed to search out and destroy Ebola cells. To control these nanobots, we will insert a programmed microchip under the skin of the patient and the hunter-killer teams will be paired electronically with the microchip. Each installation of chip and hunter-killer teams will be programmed to become part of the host body and react to that body's needs with regard to negating the Ebola virus cells. We are also designing the chip to have capability to link into a mobile phone data network so that medical staff can monitor the progress of the vaccine and ensure the hunter-killer teams are working on the targeted cells.'

Zhang Jin continued after a short pause for breath. 'We can use the existing mobile phone data networks in more developed countries to read data and send instructions to the chip if those data networks are of the right quality, but for less developed areas we will need to install our own reliable data systems.'

Wang Hu slumped back in his chair, and that is the technical crux of this solution, notwithstanding the possible objections of inserting microchips into human beings, particularly when those chips are capable of communication with the outside world. Still, be chipped or be dead? It would seem an easy choice, but there will be those who will object.

Zhang Jin continued. 'We have constructed the first of the nanobots, paired them to the first programmed microchips and tested them for communication in laboratory conditions. We have also gone further and tested a pairing on a laboratory fruit bat infected with a strain of Ebola. The microchip was programmed to focus the hunter-killer teams onto the Ebola virus cells two days ago, and it looks like we have cleared the virus. If we are to get this developed quickly then we need to identify a human host now so that we can run the experiment.'

Zhang Jin paused again. 'There is one more thing, which I have not yet mentioned.'

'Oh, what is that Zhang Jin?' said Wang Hu.

'There is only one metal that works with the semiconductor base and organic compound, and that is able to be injected into the human body without causing adverse reaction in this type of application, and there is only one substance which we can use to coat the exterior of each nanobot to protect it from the immune system.' He paused.

'Go on.' said Wang Hu.

'Gold for the metallic base and diamond for the exterior crust, and we will need a lot of it.' said Zhang Jin abruptly. 'I would suggest a lot more than we can recycle out of old computers.'

The Solution. June 2021.

To test or not to test that is the question.

For the fifth time that week Professor Wang Hu and Doctor Zhang Jin sat in front of the Crisis Committee of the Chinese Government. The atmosphere was tense. The committee chairman was Wang Chen, a middle height, powerful looking man with the trademark jet black hair cut in the accepted government style. The other six members had similar looks and managed to project an aura of malevolent intimidation towards Wang Hu and Zhang Jin. Wang Hu reflected on the benefit of having the most common surname in China, everyone may suspect they were related, but in reality Wang Hu and Wang Chen were not. That tenuous surname connection was not helping him here. This was crunch time.

Wang Chen spoke, loudly and clearly. 'Professor, we have focussed great effort on getting your solution to this point. You have had everything that you have requested, at the same time has we have diverted resource from other potentially promising projects. Our people are now dying in numbers, which it is difficult to imagine or sustain. The people are looking to us in the government to save them. They have faith that we will. Yet you are here in front of me, telling me that you are not ready to release the vaccine. Why?'

Wang Hu gathered his strength for one more effort to get what he needed. 'Wang Chen, we have had much success in proving the vaccine in animal hosts against this strain of the Ebola virus. We have had only two tests in human cases. Both cases were infected Chinese nationals which you allocated to us to test our vaccine. As you know, our vaccine relies on the controlled replication of the nanobots within the human body, to ensure we have the density to defeat the Ebola virus cells, and also depends upon the protective coating of the nanobots to ensure that the immune system of the human body does not destroy the nanobots before they can do their job. In the first test, we could not control the replication, and we discovered that we had an error in the coding of the chip inserted into the subject. The nanobots essentially were replicating, uncontrolled and within a short space of time attacking any cells, healthy or otherwise, within the body of the test case. This was all in my report to you.'

'But you solved this problem with more accurate programming of the chip, yes?' interjected Wang Chen.

Wang Hu noted the lack of concern regarding the eventual outcome for the test subject. It was not pretty and Wang Hu was still having nightmares about the event. The test team had to terminate the life of the subject, to be clear, to kill the subject, in order to prevent the nanobot vaccine from destroying him slowly cell by cell. He guessed that in the mind of Wang Chen this was just the death of one person, weighed against the potential for the death of the Chinese nation, indeed all of humanity.

Wang Hu continued. 'Yes, we identified the coding problems and re-worked a new program and tried this against an infected test case ape.'

'That was successful, yes?'

'Yes.' Wang Hu moved on with his narrative. 'We moved on to the second test subject one week later. In this case the vaccine began working, and the nanobots began actively seeking and destroying Ebola cells. We monitored via the microchip inserted within the subject and all appeared to be going well with the required replication of nanobots occurring in a controlled manner.'

'But?' questioned Wang Chen.

'Within 12 hours of insertion the nanobots began to be inactive. The subject died within another 3 hours.' said Wang Hu. 'An autopsy was performed immediately, under strict isolation protocols, and we discovered that the nanobots had been destroyed by the immune system. It seemed our outer casing diamond formula was not strong enough for continued performance within the human body. Our teams have since looked at this and discovered that the diamond protective casing was not the issue. It was in fact the bonding formula used to keep the nanobot inside its casing. This is what the immune system exploited. We have now implemented a re-designed formula, and need to test this on a human case.'

Wang Chen stood up and paced around behind the committee table. 'So, let me sum up. Two human test subjects, and two failures. I have read the very thorough and compelling reports into both tests and you are assuring me that you have solved both issues. Are you clear that this next test of the vaccine will be successful, and you will be in a position to start production and release of the vaccine within the month?'

'Wang Chen, we are in a position to conduct the test, and we are confident in our work, but this will still only be one test and we will have to conduct a full range of tests before release.' responded Wang Hu.

'You misunderstand me Wang Hu. I was not asking you a question. You will have one more chance to try this. One more subject will be released to you. Just one more person for you to try to save: or to die in important service of the country and humanity. You are aware that these subjects are not volunteers for testing? No? You will make this test a success, and you will ensure that our Chinese scientists and medical experts are seen to be saving humanity. The theory of the vaccine is sound, you have said so yourself. Make this work in practice, and leave the mass production and distribution of the vaccine to our industry. There will be no more test cases.'

Wang Hu sat back, shattered by the onslaught of Wang Chen.

Wang Chen moved closer to Wang Hu and Zhang Jin. He pointed forcefully in the direction of both. 'You will make this happen. Be under no illusion, if this test is a failure, our latest government figures indicate that we will not be in any sort of position to be providing other human lab rats for further tests. Our calculations tell us that if we have not begun a successful program to produce workable vaccines within the next month, then we will not have time to effectively deploy them. I'm sure you already know this.'

Wang Chen moved back to his seat and sat down heavily.

Zhang Jin leapt to his feet. 'You know, Wang Chen, what is required to get vaccines properly tested and licensed. You know that what we have been doing only just enters the Clinical Development phase. You know that in reality we are not even close to completing Phase 1. In Phase 1a of the accepted process we are supposed to be dealing with volunteers, up to 100, for testing. As you have pointed out we have only been receiving test cases selected by your committee from the general population. We are not even close to moving to the next Phase and onto licensing. Without the proper testing we could get this very wrong.'

Wang Chen took a few seconds to gather his thoughts and replied in a measured tone. 'Zhang Jin, sit down please and let me explain what your government needs you to do. You have been instrumental in bringing forward an extremely advanced, imaginative and innovative solution to a problem that threatens the entire human race on this earth. When I, and this entire committee of eminent academics, first examined your proposal, we came to a conclusion; this is not a vaccine in the accepted sense, but more a technological solution to the Ebola virus problem. There is no other solution as close to completion as this one. Despite what you may think, we in the government have not been idle while you and your colleagues were working hard to test your findings. When we first took account of the nature of your invention, we realised that this could be fast tracked as a technology based solution and not a solution simply based on the identification of antigens required to create immune responses in the body. As you yourself must be aware, this is a completely new way of doing medicine! You know this. You must know also that this opens the way for a different approach to development of the cure.'

Zhang Jin sat back in his chair and tried to assimilate what Wang Chen was saying. This idea had been in his head, but he had put this to the very back of his mind. As an extremely competent, dedicated scientist he was aware of the strict rules and testing regimes required in the development of all medicines.

Wang Chen continued. 'So, this government has not been idle. We have been in discussion with the US FDA and the WHO since the very beginning of this project. They have recognised the difference of this injected vaccine, to any other vaccine previously developed. Given the situation the world finds itself in, the FDA and WHO have effectively agreed for us to progress development of your vaccine at the fastest possible speed, using whatever testing regime we see fit. There will be no other chances.'

Wang Chen let this information sink in, then he continued.

'We did not inform you of this background before, because we suspected you would be more comfortable working within your normal scientific testing regime, in the knowledge that you were being fully supported by this government, and by collaborations with the USA and WHO. Things must now move as fast as possible. You have all that you require. You must ensure the next test case is successful, and you must be ready to pass to us full scale production of the vaccine before the end of this month. We will then do the rest. Is that understood?'

Wang Hu knew the current regulations required much more extensive testing for large scale use of new medicines, but in his heart he also knew Wang Chen was right. This was a different form of medicine, perhaps capable of a much faster timeline to use, once the initial batch had proved successful. This test was the last chance to demonstrate the vaccine in practice. It was essentially the last chance saloon for humanity. Deals had been struck between the Chinese and US governments to produce and deploy the vaccine once it was ready. Production of the nanobots, microchips and supporting IT infrastructure was all to be done in China by a new China and USA owned Joint Venture company; named Zhang Medical Systems, in honour of Doctor Zhang Jin, the creator of the vaccine. It would not make Doctor Zhang Jin rich of course, after all this was still China and all the revenues would go into government coffers. Deployment of the vaccines was to be coordinated by US Medicare Companies under the auspices of the World Health Organisation. It seemed like a neat arrangement, and it may just work. The USA had even donated significant gold and diamond resources for use in the production of the nanobots.

Only one problem seemed to stand in the way, successful testing of the vaccine. This was the last chance.

The Solution. June 2021.

The Final Test

Wang Chen was true to his word. By the time Wang Hu and Zhang Jin were back in the Beijing Medical Research Institute at 3pm, the paperwork for a new test case was on the system. As usual no name given, just the medical information needed to conduct the vaccine test. Unbelievably quick and efficient even for China. Wang Hu and Zhang Jin went to work quickly; Zhang Jin assembling his expert team, Wang Hu ensuring the requisite protective measures were put in place for the research establishment as a whole and for his colleagues in the testing laboratory. This was a routine they had perfected over the last months, and when the test case was rolled into the specially fitted out Ebola laboratory the team would be assembled in their protective clothing with all the equipment they needed to implement the testing procedure.

More information arrived on the system; the test case was due to arrive from the Beijing General Hospital at 4pm. Wang Hu called Zhang Jin , told him the news and set the time for the team to assemble in the test laboratory at 4:30pm. Zhang Jin confirmed that the team would be ready with the test vaccine and its associated equipment before that time. Wang Hu began the short walk from his office to the test laboratory preparation room. Zhang Jin was already there.

'All set?' asked Wang Hu.

Zhang Jin responded. 'Yes, the team is assembled in the lab, and the latest version of the nanobot vaccine is ready. We have been through all the medical notes and the microchip is programmed for the test case and paired to the nanobot vaccine. Our microchip monitor is set up to receive immediate readings and to send commands to the nanobots if necessary.'

Wang Hu considered Zhang Jin closely. He was only 35 years old, but he looked to have aged significantly over the past few months. He was thin and sallow looking, hardly surprising as he had rarely ventured outside of the Research Institute offices and laboratories since the crisis began. He had no doubts that the power of Zhang Jin's mind would carry him through the punishing schedule of work they had accepted, he just hoped his body would keep up. I guess we all look very tired, he thought. They scrubbed up and then suited up. Once they had checked the secure fittings of all of the protective suiting segments they walked through the airlock and into the controlled environment of the test laboratory. No time to waste now, just get straight on with the task.

Wang Hu looked around the laboratory. He expected to see two other suited up individuals in the lab, members of Zhang Jin's extended team to assist in the process, but there were four. Looking through the mask of the first one, he saw the grim face of Wang Chen. Clearly he was intent on this test receiving his personal attention. Clearly there was also the chance of instant admonishment should things go wrong. The second individual was significantly taller, and when he looked closely through the mask he saw a distinctly, white, Caucasian type of face staring back at him. He had the impression that the stranger may be American. He didn't know why, just something about his look and upright stance.

No time for introductions, Wang Chen simply said, 'We are here to observe. Please carry on.'

Zhang Jin and Wang Hu exchanged a quick glance, gave

a shrug and then simply began their checks of the motionless person. No time for following the normal pleasantries of laboratory etiquette. The test case was stretched out on the laboratory table, fluids and other medications flowing into his body via the type of lines you would see in normal operating theatres. One canula, inserted into the left arm was left open to receive the vaccine container. His blood pressure, heart rate and respiratory rate, displayed on the laboratory equipment, were all within range for the test to begin. The team had worked quickly to have all this in place, but then everybody knew this was a matter of life and death for this particular human, and potentially all others.

The un-named person on the table was fully sedated, motionless, breathing slowly. One more thing he noticed immediately, he was white, Caucasian looking, not Chinese. Wang Hu observed he looked at peace, but he knew this virulent strain of Ebola was coursing savagely through his body and would subject him to a slow, agonising death if this vaccine did not work. He was not religious, but, all the same, he uttered a silent prayer before signalling the team to begin the administration of the vaccine.

Zhang Jin stepped forward to the table, took hold of the left hand of the test case and placed it palm first onto a slightly elevated shelf. His assistant, a junior doctor from Beijing General Hospital called Lijuan, cleaned the top of the hand then made a small incision, between the second and third finger just above the wrist. Zhang Jin took a small package from the instrument trolley beside him, unpacked it, then brought down his magnifying glasses into his eye-line and, using extremely delicate medical tweezers picked up the tiny microchip and placed it in the incision in the left hand of the test case.

He then pushed the microchip deeper into the incision and

called to Wang Hu. 'Please test the connection of the microchip with the data reader.'

This was the first critical phase. The microchip inserted must immediately attract electrical impulses from the subject's brain to activate its systems. Without this electrical impulse the chip would have no power. Wang Hu waited. It seemed like an eternity, but in fact only seconds, continually checking the tablet computer on the small desk beside him. A chime from the tablet prompted Wang Hu to respond. 'The device is recognised and sending data to the reader'.

Stage one completed, Lijuan inserted a small suture on the incision and Zhang Jin moved on to the next task. The second assistant, one of Zhang Jin's more senior researchers, stood by with a small metal container. He opened the container and extracted a short thin, glass tube with a needle at the end. Without hesitating he passed this to Zhang Jin, who immediately inserted the needle into the open canula in the left arm of the subject. Carefully and deliberately he injected the fluid contained in the tube. He then removed the tube and placed it back into the container, which his assistant then closed up.

Zhang Jin looked intently at Wang Hu, who was looking just as intently at the tablet screen. There was an audible ping from the tablet. Wang Hu lifted his head and nodded towards Zhang Jin. 'Paired.' he said.

Zhang Jin gave an audible sigh of relief and stepped back from the table.

The un-named white male spoke for the first time, in a clear US accent. 'What now?'

Zhang Jin stepped in. 'Now we wait'.

'How long?' said the American.

'As long as it takes, but if our modifications all work as they should, we ought to have some results to report within three hours.' responded Zhang Jin.

'And if not?' he persisted.

'Then we will have failed.' interjected Wang Hu.

The team began the process of preparing the test case for longer term monitoring as Wang Chen and the American departed from the test laboratory, through the airlock.

The Solution. June 2021.

The Release

It was 7 hours since the injection of the nanobot serum into the final test case, the last chance. Wang Hu was dozing in his office chair, adjusted back to provide an almost completely flat bed. Zhang Jin had not slept. In fact he had not really slept for months. All his waking, and dozing hours, had been filled with solving this problem, this existential problem for humanity. He had virtually lived in his office and the laboratory, only occasionally returning to his small bachelor flat in Beijing centre. Usually when he got home he realised there was something else he needed to follow up and duly returned to his office within a couple of hours. Now, as they approached the culmination of his work, he admitted to himself that he was feeling unbearably tired and overwhelmed, but his brain and body continued running on adrenalin and copious infusions of coffee.

In his mind he was continually replaying each stage of the process; the identification of the Ebola cells for destruction, the nanobot and microchip design and production, the programming process, the intricacies of the computer program itself, the invention of the carrier fluid to transport the nanobot hunter-killer teams into the bloodstream and provide sufficient raw material particles to allow replication of the nanobots, and, finally, the design and production of the supporting IT system. Yes, the IT system, the all important key to maintaining control of the nanobots once inserted into the human body. Everything he and his teams had worked on was equally critical to the development of this answer to the Ebola, but it was the IT aspects and the overall rushed development of the vaccine that worried him most of all. He had thought himself crazy when he first came up with this idea, but there were no possibilities identified to create a traditional antigen based vaccine that would kill this particularly nasty strain of Ebola. Normal strains were bad enough, but this one! This was a real judgement day plague inflicted on humanity, but by a malignant God figure, or perhaps by a planet trying to defend itself from ever encroaching human enterprise? Who knew? Certainly not Zhang Jin, he just focussed himself on providing the solution; and provide a solution he had, even though it seemed like something straight out of science fiction. Still, he must have faith in his own work and in the work of his expert colleagues, perhaps also in the work of Wang Chen and his committee. After all, he thought, surely we all have the same aim in this, the saving of mankind?

Zhang Jin thought that he really should sleep while they waited for the vaccine to start producing the results they thought possible. Instead he wandered one more time to the coffee machine and poured himself a large black coffee. He took a sip and, as the hot coffee began to re-vitalise his thought processes once more, he ran through the factors that still worried him. In the first test the program to control the replication and targeting of the nanobots had failed and they had essentially attacked every cell in the subject's body. He still had nightmares over the fact that they had to terminate the life of the subject, a young Chinese construction worker, before he was destroyed piece by piece from the inside. He was a scientist and he had been forced to kill another human being. So, the team had re-evaluated the program and created more specific rules for the nanobots; only allowing replication to a level needed to assist in destroying the specified

Ebola cells, and ensuring other cells were left in the condition they were found in. They could never inject sufficient nanobots into the bloodstream at one go, so it was essential that some replication was allowed to ensure enough were present to do the job, but not too many. He reflected that he should have thought more carefully about this before the first test, but they were being pushed forward at breakneck speed by circumstance. The second problem of bonding the protective coating of each nanobot, which caused the failure of the second test, had been resolved quickly, and was now not concerning him. If all went well with the control of nanobots, once inserted for a long period into the human body, then the solution should be proved.

He took another sip of his coffee and tried to settle his mind. Zhang Jin took his smartphone out of the top pocket of his lab coat and checked the output figures again, for what seemed like the hundredth time that night. The team had also developed a good, usable and readable application for their smartphones. The app enabled the team to read the outputs directly from the chip reader in the laboratory, so they knew the instant any change occurred. He scanned the current readings and made a mental note; no changes yet, but the subject did not seem to be getting worse. Well, that had to be a good sign. He went back to his desk and began working through the coding of the program once again. After 30 minutes intensely scrutinising each line of code, he was as sure as he could be that there were no more possible glitches with the programming.

Zhang Jin sat back in his chair, took a sip of his long cold coffee and closed his eyes for a second. He began drifting into a sort of half-sleeping, half-awake state. A not unpleasant sensation of relaxation came across him, but he was then jerked awake by an alarm tone from his smart phone. He ignored it, and tried to stay in this sate of relaxation, but the phone continued its chirps, which became more insistent with every repetition of the jangly tone. Zhang Jin dragged himself back to full consciousness as he realised that the tone was indicating changed readings from the test. He began to look at the readings at the same time as his phone rang.

When he answered it was Lijuan, speaking excitedly. ‘Zhang Jin you need to get in here quickly. There is a change in the readings and we are taking new blood samples now. You will want to oversee this no doubt.’

He looked more closely at the readings on his app, raised blood pressure, previously accelerated activity from the nanobot teams was beginning to drop, good respiratory progress and body temperature hitting normal levels. This was looking promising. Zhang Jin spoke quickly, ‘Lijuan, do not take the blood samples yet. We need to wait until the readings indicate that the nanobot activity has slowed down to negligible levels. Just wait, I will wake the Professor and we will be with you within 15 minutes.’

He continued to monitor the app readings as he ran into Wang Hu’s office. He shook the sleeping professor violently, and dragged him to his feet. ‘We need to get back into the laboratory now, Professor.’ he said as he pulled the half-asleep Wang Hu towards the office door and out into the corridor leading to the laboratory. Wang Hu may have been 65 years old but he did not show it as he moved from deep sleep to wide-awake in the space of 5 seconds, and began to move quickly towards the laboratory. They did not take time suiting up, but stood in the isolated observation gallery, Zhang Jin monitoring the readings on his smart phone. He hit the communication button. ‘Lijuan, the level of nanobot activity seems to be dropping down now, we should see this drop to nothing within the next minutes. At that point take the blood samples.' Lijuan signalled to Zhang Jin that she understood.

Zhang Jin watched the readings drop, and after two minutes of scrutiny said to Lijuan, 'OK, take the samples now.'

The first of the sample bottles was already inserted into the canula and Lijuan began to draw off blood from the subject. Zhang Jin and Wang Hu moved to the airlock area of the laboratory and began to suit up. In record time they were properly suited and into the laboratory, just in time to see Lijuan draw off the fourth and final sample. The samples were then moved to the blood testing station in the laboratory and Zhang Jin began to run each sample through the battery of tests devised to detect the Ebola virus. No need for external verification of this process, just the need to get this done quickly, but accurately and properly. As Zhang Jin continued the testing process, Wang Hu entered the results into the test database they had put together some weeks before. As each individual reading was entered, the indicators and figures in the database moved from Red to Green colouring. All looking good so far, Wang Hu even dared to begin hoping that they had been successful at last.

Wang Chen and the American appeared at the observation window. Wang Chen hit the intercom button. 'What is happening?' he bellowed into the microphone.

Wang Hu took stock of the results and replied. 'As we expected the nanobot activity has receded to zero, life signs are stable and we are now about to test the final blood sample taken from the patient some 30 minutes ago. So far it looks like we are receiving very positive readings from the blood. It is now all down to the results from the last blood sample. Please be patient for just a few more minutes.'

Wang Hu noticed that Wang Chen had switched off the intercom, and that the American was addressing Wang Chen in an animated fashion.

Zhang Jin continued in an unhurried fashion. He was excited, but now was not the time to cut corners and record false results. Everything depended upon this process being clear of error. He finished the testing and read the final readings to Wang Hu. The database indicators showed all green. Zhang Jin wanted to scream aloud with relief, but Wang Hu broke his delirious thoughts with a polite but firm request to check back through each input. All the figures were verified correct and Zhang Jin stood back from the test bench. The energy suddenly drained from his body, he collapsed onto a nearby chair and leaned forward holding his suddenly heavy head in his hands.

Wang Chen once again activated the intercom, saying, 'What is wrong? Another failure?'

The professor shook his head slowly. 'Not at all Wang Chen, the blood samples are all clear. There are no Ebola cells, the vaccine has worked!'

Wang Hu could see that the suited figure of Zhang Jin was sobbing uncontrollably as he sat leaning forward on the chair.

'Well done, we can take this from here.' said Wang Chen. He noticed Wang Chen and the American congratulating each other warmly as they left the observation room.

He wondered what would happen next, but quickly realised that this was no longer his problem. Wang Hu stood in the centre of the laboratory, thanked all present for their extraordinary efforts, grabbed hold of Zhang Jin and pulled him out of the laboratory.

He took no time thinking about the paucity of gratitude from Wang Chen, and it never bothered him that he still did not know the name of the American observer.

The Solution. August 2021.

The USA and China save the day

'We now have the solution.' The slide show began slickly as the newly elected Democrat President David Miles addressed the assembled national leaders. 'But before we go into detail I think we need to just recap why we are here.'

His assistant moved the slideshow on to reveal a statement:

"Here's the bottom line. Patients can beat this disease. And we can beat this disease. But we have to stay vigilant. We have to work together at every level — federal, state and local. And we have to keep leading the global response, because the best way to stop this disease, the best way to keep Americans safe, is to stop it at its source — in West Africa."

– President Obama, October 25, 2014

'You will recall that in 2014 President Obama supported a policy to contain Ebola within the African continent and work on eradicating the disease at its source. We all know that there was a significant effort from many countries to help eradicate Ebola. We all know now that the effort failed, due to an unexpected mutation in the disease itself and natural events that helped spread the new variant of the disease much further among the global population than could have been reasonably expected. Perhaps we did not remain vigilant enough. Perhaps we should have seen that the consequences of destroying natural habitat for Fruit Bats could have initiated mass migrations that would be instrumental in spreading this new variant of the virus. Perhaps we should have been maintaining a closer watch on the evolution of this virus, and anticipated that new strains were coming. Perhaps we should have been putting more effort into all of these things, and remained vigilant as President Obama said. However many times we say 'perhaps', the truth is our inactions have resulted in the situation we are in today.'

The slide show moved on, revealing, by continent and country, a truly terrible set of figures indicating the millions already dead and infected. Nobody appeared to be totally immune.

President Miles continued in his usual measured tone, pointing to the slide on the huge screen behind him. 'As we have all borne terrible witness to, none of our tried and tested solutions worked on this new, deadly strain. We have all suffered greatly from the rapid spread of this new variant of Ebola.' He let the figures sink in, then carried on with his narrative, 'Well, I am here today to tell you that we believe we have a new vaccine that will be effective against this new strain of Ebola. We, the USA and China, have been working secretly over the past months to put together an extremely innovative solution to this terrible disease. The vaccine can be used to cure those already infected and as a preventative against the disease. You will see on your screens now the scientific basis for the vaccine, and see that the deployment of the vaccine also requires infrastructure upgrades for monitoring the progress of vaccinated people. The nature of the vaccine requires this infrastructure investment, or it will not be possible to provide vaccinations. I am sorry, but those are the conditions.'

There were a few mutterings among the assembled dignitaries, but the President either did not notice or chose to ignore them. He pushed forward with the briefing. 'We have created a USA-China Joint Venture, called Zhang Medical Systems, to produce and deploy the vaccine and its associated technologies. This Joint Venture Company also involves collaborations with all our national medical companies, large and small. During deployment of the vaccine the Joint Venture Company will be assisted fully by specialist military teams. We are serious about getting this vaccine to as many as possible, in as short a time as possible. Over the last month the vaccine has begun mass production in China and our new JV has been setting up distribution points, with the aid of our military, at various points globally. The populations of the USA and China will begin to be vaccinated at the end of this month, and we anticipate deliveries globally to begin by early September.'

The president paused for breath, now for the crunch. 'We, the USA and China, have borne the cost of developing this vaccine, and, because of the technical aspects involved, those costs have been and will continue to be high. We cannot provide vaccines to all without substantial buy in to this new Joint Venture Zhang Medical Systems. We expect national leaders to contribute significantly, as we have, and will continue to do. We will also float this company on stock exchanges East and West, from midnight tonight, to create more investment to help with continued development and deployment of the vaccine. This will be the largest medical-industrial effort on this planet, created to tackle the largest-scale medical emergency ever. A true threat to humanity, to be tackled by a truly globally responsive initiative, but you must contribute on a national level to receive the benefits. I thank you for your attention.'

President Miles stepped back slightly from the presidential podium, and took in the response; wild applause from the leaders of richer nations, dismayed looks from the poorer nations. Of course, this is what he expected, the real work would now begin; who would get the vaccine and who would not, how many doses of the vaccine would be needed? The President had anticipated that at this point in his speech the Foreign Relations Branches of both the US and Chinese Governments would be overwhelmed with requests for contacts with high level officials. Both governments had set up separate call centres to deal with this.

He stepped back to the podium, 'You will see on your screens now the contact numbers and e-mail addresses you need to become part of this vaccination program. We have set up specialist government call centres to get this project going and coordinate deployment of the vaccine. You are advised to get in contact as soon as possible. We will be moving quickly from now on. If you need any information on the technicalities of the vaccine then, I would like to point out, that we have the inventor here with us tonight, Doctor Zhang Jin. I will not be taking questions on this subject.' The president stepped fully back from the podium and exited the presentation theatre surrounded by his secret service protection squad.

Wang Hu and Zhang Jin were uncomfortably aware that many eyes now rested on them. Up until this point they had been hidden among the large Chinese Government delegation seated at the left hand side of the hall, but now they were pointed out for all to see. Zhang Jin wondered how his invention to save humanity had now effectively been turned into a benefit to only some of the human race, particularly those whose governments could buy in to the Zhang Medical Systems Joint Venture. It was good of the Chinese Government to honour him in this way, but he could not forget that his team had been working non-stop for months to bring the original idea through the proof of concept, and on into testing the prototype. All achieved at breakneck speed. From then on, the whole project had disappeared into the medical industrial plants for large scale production. Zhang Jin had effectively seen nothing of the vaccine since that time, but he hoped that further testing had occurred along the production path. He thought that maybe he should not worry too much, after all he and all the research teams in the Beijing Medical Research Facility had volunteered to be the first to be vaccinated, using the vaccine as a preventative measure against the Ebola, and everything had worked fine. No side effects, the nanobot hunter-killer teams had remained inactive having found no Ebola cells. They would immediately activate if cells were detected in the future. Still, he had pursued this invention to help humankind, and the statement from the President of the USA, supported by his own government, clearly indicated that deployment of the vaccine could only occur in contributing nations. He hoped that this was just political speak to solicit some help from the poorer nations and that they would not just be cut off from this, the only method of killing of this Ebola virus strain. He was also not sure how he felt about the whole thing being turned into some giant capitalist medical company, but he had been assured by Wang Chen that this was the way to get his vaccine out into the world with the best possible speed. He had to believe Wang Chen had all their interests at heart; he was a member of the Chinese Communist Party after all, not a capitalist. Zhang Jin put these thoughts to the back of his mind and awaited the expected onslaught of questions.

As he made his way back to his armoured limousine, the President hoped his presentation had worked and that other national leaders would want to buy the safety of their nations. The huge costs involved meant that nations would have to help with some form of contribution, the USA and China alone could not be expected to save all of humanity. He also hoped that national leaders were now deep in thought on how to ensure the safety of their populations, but he also suspected that many would simply be looking at how they could benefit from shares in the new Joint Venture. His answer to that suspicion would be clearly shown on stock markets the following day, when Zhang Medical Systems shares were released onto the trading floors. Individuals bought shares and governments bought shares, in large or small amounts. Wall Street had the best day ever for trading in medical securities. Markets in the Europe and the East followed suit.

This was the way you saved humankind in the 21st Century. No heroics, just science and market forces combined.

The Solution. Autumn 2021.

View from a hospital bed

John Miles was still in the Beijing Medical Research Institute. His thoughts took him back over his story one more time. He found it difficult to believe he was still alive. He took stock of the environment, a pleasant enough room with access to phones, internet, TV and all the electronic accoutrements deemed necessary for modern day life. Although, he had not really felt the need for them in West Africa back in the early part of the year, when he had been a volunteer doctor trying desperately to save local villages from complete annihilation by the new strain Ebola, he valued their presence now. The Chinese medical folks in the Institute were always extremely courteous and helpful, but he needed the contacts with the wider world, and he longed to be back outside again.

He knew the risks when he volunteered to go to West Africa, but he had all the vaccinations and antibiotics thought to help at the time and he went anyway. He was a doctor, young, with no real responsibilities and he wanted to help. His father, then Senator David Miles, now President David Miles, had begged him to stay in the USA and not to travel at all. As sons do, John listened respectfully to his father's advice and pleas, but continued to follow his chosen path. He wanted to do something, not just sit around watching the inevitable happen. John had seen countless horrors, many people dead in the streets, many infected people gravitating to the United Nations field hospital where he was working. The saddest thing for him to cope with was that he knew nothing they could do would save these people; they were losing the fight, and losing badly. Then he remembered that after a couple of months of this he began feeling tired, but who wouldn't, he had a punishing workload. John lost all track of time, became focussed entirely on what he was doing, and did not even notice that his father had been elected President of the USA, after a snap election forced by the impeachment of the serving President. He worked day and night, barely resting, and then, one fine, sunny day, while he was still working on a patient, he closed his eyes to sleep; then he woke up here in Beijing some weeks later.

How he had got here he didn't know, but he guessed that his father now being President probably had something to do with it. What had happened to him he did not know. He only knew, from brief conversations with attending medical staff that he had been extremely lucky. He had received some experimental treatment developed here in the Beijing Medical Research Institute, and it had been totally successful. He had arrived with the new strain of the Ebola virus, and now he did not have it. He thought that without his father now being POTUS, that he probably would not be here right now, would not have had the chance to survive. He tried asking whether he could now leave and go back to the USA, but the answer was always the same; orders for the Institute were to keep him here until told otherwise. John guessed that they were just maintaining observations on him, to make sure the new treatment had no side effects. That would seem good practice.

So, he settled down to building up his fitness in the rather superb Institute gym, following the news and catching up with his father, mother and sister by phone and social media. As he said to his father, he actually felt very well, well enough to be released, although he felt like he had been asleep for a hundred years. In any case he decided to just do as he was told and wait.

As an exercise for his still groggy brain over the ensuing months he began to piece together and follow what was happening. As far as he could make out, he had been a test case for the vaccine developed here in the Institute, by Chinese medical research scientists. John could not find any reference to other test cases, which he found strange. He found an electronic copy of his father's speech at the national leaders' meeting in August. Very good, but wow, what a statement, contribute to this new Joint Venture or don't receive the vaccine! Unfortunately, he could not find the associated pack of scientific information that was available for the delegates. So, he knew whatever the vaccine was it had apparently worked on him, but he did not know exactly how. He could see from reports that the vaccination program was well advanced in the USA and China, but he noted that for some reason, outlying areas of China, such as the Xinjiang region were not figuring in reports of the program's implementation progress. It seemed China was intent on keeping its own progress to itself. Well, other countries had their own problems to be concerned with. Delivery of the vaccine and its associated infrastructure had begun in Europe, and the United Nations and the Vatican had joined forces to embarrass the USA and China to begin deploying the vaccine in Africa, the Middle East and India where the spread of the virus was continuing to accelerate. The Vatican was reportedly bringing together a coalition of world religions and using some of their combined wealth to ensure poorer nations were being bought into the program. This had all happened at lightning speed, and was bringing real hope to humankind. Well, at least to those who were able to access official information sources. Those who couldn't, he guessed, were simply just living in fear and waiting for their turn to be struck down by the virus.

He had not been aware of such USA-China collaboration in developing the vaccine, and what was this about the infrastructure? What sort of infrastructure was needed, and turning this whole program into a business, what was that all about?

He continued to follow the reports as he remained cooped up in the Institute, enduring test after test. Still, a small price to pay, being alive, when he could have been very dead, he thought. As the weeks progressed deep into autumn he began to sense in his father's tone during their telephone calls that the worst was over for the USA. Reports he was reading online bore this out and by the end of November the USA and China officially declared their vaccination programs complete. Their populations clear of Ebola. By the middle of December the World Health Organisation was reporting that globally, all who had been included in the program had received vaccinations and regions had declared themselves clear of the Ebola virus.

It would seem the global catastrophe was over.

John had continued a regime of fitness training and generally keeping his mind alert and he finally received clearance from the Institute to go home to the USA in the middle of December. No more tests required and he would be back well in time for Christmas. He felt fitter and healthier than he could ever remember, and made a mental note that he had not even had a cold over the past couple of months.

He could not wait to get back to the USA to celebrate Christmas and New Year with his family, get back into the usual routine at the George Washington University Hospital and put all of the events of the last year behind him.

Book 2

Blessing or Curse?

Everything we love about civilization is a product of intelligence, so amplifying our human intelligence with artificial intelligence has the potential of helping civilization flourish like never before – as long as we manage to keep the technology beneficial.

Humanity's saviour

Or is it?

Medical research scientists and experts world-wide were worried. Why should that be? The results coming back from use of the new vaccine proved that it worked effectively. The new Ebola strain seemed to be eradicated in the human population of this sorely pressed Earth. Well, in that part of the world's population that had received the vaccinations anyway. There were still no real plans to investigate those remote, controlled areas where it is known the vaccine did not reach. Was everybody dead in there, or had some groups of people managed to escape the global spread of this vicious virus? Nobody really knew, and no governments or non-governmental organisations seemed to be asking questions? Worse still, it seemed that some governments had closed all access, physical and electronic, to certain regions. It seemed that everyone who had survived was simply hoping that now the whole thing had gone away. Nobody questioned governments about what had gone on within their own national borders during the deployment of the vaccine. Journalists, researchers and medical organisations had initially asked questions of national governments, but had firstly been politely rebuffed, and then, if they persisted, been forcefully told to not ask such questions. A number of persistent investigators around the world had even been imprisoned, or had frankly just disappeared from public view.

Was it this that concerned health experts and scientists? Not really, they accepted that what had to be done to preserve humanity, had been done. After all, they themselves were beneficiaries, they were still alive! They had gladly accepted the chance to be vaccinated, even overcoming their own Human Rights concerns about being 'chipped'. Better chipped like their pets than dead.

No, a number of details concerned the scientists, first among them the scientific purity of the development process. In particular, the lack of publicly available technical data about the development and testing of the vaccine was a concern to the scientific community. To be frank, the data packs presented during President Miles's speech all those months ago had been sparse in technical detail; particularly sparse regarding the testing and licensing regime for the vaccine. Numerous scientists had been working on developing nanobot medicines for years. Indeed the first nanoparticle based medicine had been approved for use way back in 1995, but developing nanobots of the type outlined in this approach? Research Institutes in the USA had long imagined the idea of diagnostic nanobots able to roam around the human body detecting and repairing damaged cells, but the process for developing and testing was known to be extremely long and onerous, while other more traditional methods of treating disease marched along a quicker route to licensing. Part of the problem in this approach was, in fact, getting enough organic material to test on, and, the FDA being the FDA, without a rigorous test regime being applied to plentiful organic samples, the concepts would not achieve licence in the end. Scientists in this field of research wondered how sufficient testing of the new wonder cure had been completed to satisfy national licensing organisations. Indeed, did this even matter anymore, and was there already in place a new testing regime?

Still, there was an existential crisis for humanity underway and nobody cared at the time; vaccinate or die! So the world, or at least its national leaderships, chose to be vaccinated.

Even subsequent questioning of the Chinese scientists who developed the vaccine revealed nothing. Any enquiry to them was carefully screened by USA and Chinese governmental organisations. Sometimes there was an answer to a question, generally not. No information whatsoever on the testing phases, numbers involved in tests, or the results of those tests, was ever released to the scientific community. So, the situation was the world had to accept that a solution had been found, a solution that worked. Even so, the lack of available information meant that medical practitioners around the globe had no idea what side effects to plan for. All drugs have some side effects, right? The official message on this; No need to worry, everything is being monitored by the Zhang Medical Systems Artificial Intelligence system backed up by the biggest super computer data repositories ever built! Any problem would be immediately identified and a solution equally quickly implemented. So, why the constant concerns and questions from persistent doubters, why the continual concerns and queries? No need, for this, just be thankful, we have survived.

No further explanations given, and so eventually nobody continued to ask, apart from an inquisitive few with a strange tendency to disappear.

Then, of course, that brings the spotlight on the second thing that concerned scientists; Zhang Medical Systems, the whole organisation itself.

Zhang Medical Systems within months of its inception had become the largest and most powerful organisation on the planet. This joint venture of the USA and Chinese governments was untouchable in any sense. Questions went in, no information came out. Infrastructure and software up-dates all emerged without warning and were implemented under military supervision. Do not question, just let the teams do what they need to do, was the order to medical staff in all institutions. Zhang Medical Systems, ZMS for short throughout the world now, assured everybody that their systems, unlike other IT systems, were infallible, driven by the best ever AI, continuing to ensure the health of all vaccine and chip recipients. What was there to be scared of? Just trust! Why would anyone need to question the legitimacy of this organisation's actions when it was backed fully by the two greatest nations on Earth, the USA and China? Just trust that this is what humankind needed to develop in order to survive into the future.

Trust? Well, yes, but for scientific communities it was difficult to trust without verifiable data. For instance, there had been some stories of microchip insertions that had gone wrong and the vaccine had then not worked. Only stories, no official statements, no data from test cases. Stories that research scientists in China, working on production of the vaccine had developed some mysterious reaction and died. Again only stories, no official statements, no data for scientists to analyse. Stories that the original developer of the vaccine Dr Zhang, had in fact committed suicide, or even been executed by the Chinese Government. He had not been seen for some time, although Chinese news articles often carried photographs, old photographs of him, alongside the occasional official briefings given by ZMS. Only stories though, which were never verifiable from official information. People like listening to and passing on stories; all the stuff of urban legends. Fake news, always laughed off by government officials; after all, everyone was now safe, why should we question? All the assertions of fake news did not stop small social media groups springing up and putting forward fantastic conspiracy theories, some even putting forward the idea that the vaccinations contained some strange concoction not belonging to this world. Yes, humankind had apparently been saved by some alien goo, dredged up from the very pits of Area 51, not by the brilliant work of human medical scientists. Stories flew around social media, each one seemingly more outlandish and insane than the last, largely ignored by governments, who were content with the apparent paucity of scientific rigour applied to the development of the vaccine.

So, the situation was this, ZMS, deliverers of the vaccine that saved humankind from destruction by Ebola virus, and providers of the ultimate and infallible IT system to manage, control and maintain the 'cure'. That is the world's view of Zhang Medical Systems, the paternal organisation that was created and exists only for our benefit, and is answerable only to… who?

Many would say that is good enough, and we should not question, but purist scientists had one final concern. Why did the infallible IT system fail globally a number of times after midnight GMT on 31 December 2021; some sort of delayed millennium bug?

No answers given, no official statements were made. Shares in Zhang Medical Systems continued to fly on the world's trading floors, the most amazing and sustained rise ever seen in stock markets. Many funds and individual investors made fortunes, and everyone, well almost everyone, was happy.

1 January 2022

A Small Miracle?

Tony Romanov slowly awoke from his blissful doze. He was in the A&E duty bunk, where he had crashed out at about 2am. New Years Day, great, another year of hard grind ahead. He looked at the clock on the bedside cabinet. The red digits blinked at him, 0700. Strange, he had managed a whole 5 hours with no interruptions. Things had obviously been quiet overnight. He stretched his limbs, rolled out of the small bed, landing expertly in his shoes, and made his way to the coffee pot simmering invitingly on the small kitchen unit by the door. Tony poured himself a large mug of steaming black coffee. He took a sip of the hot liquid and sat down in the small armchair conveniently placed in front of the small TV. He hit the on switch of the remote and selected a random news channel. Continuing to sip his coffee, he watched as various items of news were related by the news reader. The usual stuff, Syrian conflict kicking off again, more bombing of remaining isolated rebel positions, who would think that after last year's disaster there would be a continuation of the fighting; some things are obviously more important than life itself to some people. He wondered how the rebels fighting against the Syrian state were still alive? How had they managed to get the Ebola vaccinations? Who had included them in their national program? A bit of a mystery, but somebody must have. It was well known that anybody in the middle-Eastern area who had not received the vaccination had not survived. The news moved on, President Miles giving a news conference on the introduction of new healthcare provisions for the poor in the USA. Well done, thought Tony, about time there was a more human approach to health-care in the USA. The final big story, the UK Unity Government, working over the Christmas holiday because of public pressure, introduced a new bill to re-engage with European Union officials, to try and repair the damage caused to trade and political relations over the last couple of years. Thankfully back to relatively normal news. Good to see the days of the headlines being dominated by huge death tolls caused by the Ebola outbreak seemed to be over. Tony turned off the TV, took a last gulp of his coffee and headed through the door back into A&E.

He threw a quick glance at the patient numbers on the board, looked like a very quiet night, only a couple patients with drink induced injuries being treated. He checked that everything was being taken care of and that the off-going team was ready to hand over to the on-coming shift and then he headed off to his day job in the oncology ward of the hospital. It was a bit of a walk to the ward. As he ascended the central stairwell he took the opportunity to check his smartphone for messages. The usual New Years good wishes from friends and family, all commiserating with him for having to be at work in the hospital rather than partying with them. Tony smiled to himself, to be frank, he would sooner be here!

He pushed through the double doors and entered the oncology ward. He had a number of patients under his supervision here, one in particular he needed to check in with as early as possible. Jack Childs, age 52, pancreatic cancer sufferer. He had been treated in the hospital for the past 5 months and his last MRI scan 7 days ago had indicated that the tumour on his bile duct had reached a critical mass. No treatment they had given appeared to have made any impact and the outlook did not look good. Jack was in for MRI scanning first thing this morning and Tony wanted to be there to wish Jack well, be around to assist in the interpretation of the scan and be there to give out the expected bad news. Pancreatic cancer was always the silent killer, and if there was further growth of the tumour, then all the hospital would be able to do at this point would be to arrange palliative care. No further treatment would be possible.

Tony headed towards the ward sisters desk. 'Good morning Joan.' he said. 'Any overnight items?'

'Everything has been very quiet, Doctor,' responded Joan. 'The only issue was an IT failure just after midnight. The systems dropped out completely for a short while, but I contacted the help desk straight away and they assured me they had the problem in hand. We had all systems back within about 30 minutes. There seem to be no residual problems from this.'

Tony was surprised. 'IT failure? That's the first time since the new systems were installed. Let's hope that's not the way 2022 is going to be!'

'The helpdesk people were very apologetic and had things up and running very quickly. They have asked me to make an inventory of all the current operational systems and note any on-going problems from the failure. I haven't found any so far.' Joan returned to her work, the very model of medical efficiency.

'OK, Joan. Thank you. Has Mister Childs been prepared for his MRI scan this morning? Do you know if he has been comfortable overnight?' he enquired.

Joan answered quickly. 'Mister Childs is ready Doctor. I checked him myself about 30 minutes ago. He seems to be comfortable, although he complained of a short burning sensation in the general abdomen area about three hours ago. It subsided quickly, and no problem reported since then.'

Tony left the sisters desk and moved towards Jack in Bed 5 of the ward. As he approached Jack, the porters arrived to wheel Jack to the MRI suite.

Jack caught sight of Tony and shouted, 'Hello Doc, I'm off for my scan now. Looking forward to the good news, Doc, don't let me down now! I've still got a season ticket at the Spurs to use up, and I don't anticipate missing any games.'

Tony was always impressed by the positive mental attitude of Jack. Like many Brits he was obsessed with soccer and he had been a Spurs supporter ever since his Dad had carried him to his first game. Only one year old then, and Jack maintained he had never missed a Spurs game since that day. By a great stroke of misfortune he had actually been one of the relatively few UK citizens to contract the Ebola virus. As a result he had been among the first to receive the new Zhang Medical Systems vaccination, pushed for by Tony, and the results had been entirely positive. Ebola cells cleared completely within hours. Tony was impressed beyond belief and became an overnight evangelist for accelerating and widening the vaccination program within the hospital. None of this could help weeks later when Jack received his diagnosis of Pancreatic cancer; totally unexpected. Still, Jack had proudly marked his left hand microchip insertion with a very noticeable skull and crossbones tattoo. This was absolutely typical of his sense of humour and undaunted spirit. Tony wished him well as the porters wheeled him out of the ward in the direction of the MRI scanner suite. He then settled down in the ward office, poured another coffee and began to work through the case notes of his rounds today, as he waited for the call from the MRI team.

It seemed to be an unremarkable case-load for this ward. Female, 67, ovarian cancer; Male, 65, prostate cancer; Male, 49, Lung cancer. The list went on.

It was always the youngsters that really got to him though, and in particular, he had a case now on the ward that choked him up. He looked at the case notes of a new admission, Jonathan Cleary, age 5 years; Retinoblastoma, cancer of the cells in the retina, luckily, in this case only in the left eye. He had been diagnosed only a few weeks ago and had been waiting for a bed to be free in the ward. He thought he knew the name, and then it came back to him. Jonathan had been one of a group of children he had administered the Ebola vaccine to several months back. He had remembered the worried look on Jonathan's face as he was being wheeled into theatre for the microchip insertion and vaccination, and he remembered how Jonathan had smiled and giggled when, in an effort to cheer him up, Tony had inflated a rubber glove to make it look like a chicken. The UK government had, from the start, operated a policy of vaccinating all children with the new Zhang vaccine and he had performed many of the procedures for children within range of this hospital. No exemptions had been allowed and even new-borns were vaccinated within days of birth, despite complaints of some parents. You would not believe that parents were having these life-saving vaccinations and then trying to stop vaccination of their children, because they were worried about side-effects! The fact was that children in the UK had been much luckier than children in other countries, where availability of the new vaccine was limited, either by their own governments design or due to lack of accessibility to a hospital. He took a look at the original scans of the retina and saw that the tumour was still quite small, but with the obvious potential to grow, and it had already been decided that the best treatment at this time would be Cryotherapy; a procedure to kill the cancer cells by freezing them. He made a mental note to ensure Jonathan was the first patient on his rounds.

A couple of seconds later the telephone rang. He picked it up. It was a technician from the MRI scanning team on the other end. 'Doctor Romanov, you may want to have a good look at this.' Tony quickly made his way to the MRI suite, wondering what to expect. The technician was waiting for him, Jack still lying motionless on the scanner. The MRI operator pulled up two images on the computer screen, one dated 23 December 2021, the other the current image of Jack's tumour. Tony checked the measurements with the on-screen tools, and then re-checked them. They looked at each other, taking in the information they had on the computer screen. Jack had not received any treatments since his last scan, and on that scan it was obvious that this very malignant tumour had grown aggressively and was well on the way to killing him. The image today showed no growth, indeed a reduction in the size of the tumour. Not a great reduction, but enough to be noticeable and, importantly, accurately measurable. Why that should be, he did not know, but this was a time to spread good news, and, in any case, he felt like he needed to impart some good news for once.

Tony hit the intercom button and said, 'You know Jack, you may just have got your good news. Your tumour has not grown. Indeed, it has shrunk a little. I think you might just get to see Spurs for a little while longer yet.'

From the interior of the scanner tube there came a muffled cheer, followed by an equally muffled chant of 'Come on you Spurs!' Tony laughed.

January 2022

Miracles or science?

Zhang Jin was back where he liked to be, in his laboratory, working on data. He loved data, particularly data regarding his nanobot vaccine project. He still regarded the project as his, even though the production and delivery of his miracle cure had long since been taken out of his hands and given to his commercial namesake Zhang Medical Systems. The Chinese government had wanted to continually parade Zhang Jin in front of the world's media, but he had quickly tired of that, and despite pressure from various officials, in particular Wang Chen, he had finally been allowed to return to a self-imposed seclusion deep within the Beijing Medical Research Institute. The previous couple of months, since the announcement to world leaders about the humanity-saving Ebola vaccine, created by the glorious efforts of Chinese scientists particularly Doctor Zhang Jin, and the unveiling of Zhang Medical Systems, Zhang Jin himself had become more uncomfortable and depressed. Zhang Jin knew that he, and his team, had been the ones who had created this cure. He understood that. He understood that without this scientific miracle then a good part, perhaps all, of the human race would not be alive on this planet right now. That was clear, but deep down he was feeling troubled. He was a scientist and what scientists do is test and retest theories until they are perfectly proven, or disproved. Zhang Jin knew that he, his team and Wang Hu had not done that. They had not followed the necessary testing protocols that would have ensured the safe development of the Ebola vaccine. They had not been allowed to, and, in fact, had been forced to skip vital test stages to enable the vaccine and its control programs to move into production, deployment and use. All in an obscenely short space of time. So, was this a miracle cure and perfect model of USA-China cooperation, or commercially driven potential disaster? This was the question that continually circled around his mind. Zhang Jin did not know the answer, and yet his name was there enshrined in the growing legend of Zhang Medical Systems. This concerned him on a very personal level. Was he the saviour of humanity, or could he turn out to be the catalyst of its early demise?

What concerned him most of all was not the underlying theory of the nanobot hunter-killer teams and their behaviour against Ebola virus cells. He felt sure he had that right, and Wang Hu had been clear in his critical scrutiny of the theory and practice. Wang Hu too was sure of this part of the vaccine. No, it was the issue of control of the nanobot teams once inserted in the human frame that came back to him most nights in his dreams. He vividly remembered the first live test case and how they had got the control parameters of the program so spectacularly wrong. Yes, the poor human lab rat would have died of the Ebola anyway, but the fact was they had to terminate his life themselves to prevent the nanobots running rampant through his organs. So, that was murder wasn't it? He was a scientist, a medical research scientist, who had dedicated his life so far to finding cures that kept people alive, and in this case he had intentionally killed someone. Worse, he had to terminate the life of a fellow human being, because he and his team had made errors in writing a control program, a piece of software. If only they had more time to develop and test that aspect in computer modelling prior to live testing, but there had been no time.

These test results had never been made public.

Luckily Zhang Jin had the Chinese equivalent of an angel on his shoulder, constantly looking out for him. It had become apparent to Wang Hu over the early weeks of the production and deployment of the vaccine that Zhang Jin was not handling his new found fame very well. So it was he who had worked on Wang Chen to allow Zhang Jin to step back out of the public spotlight and return to his research position. That had proved a hard task as the Chinese government wanted to permanently have on global display its scientific genius, its poster boy of innovative medicine. More than this, he also felt that they were lacking real confirmatory data, so now he was trying to rest some more concessions from Wang Chen. If he could get what he wanted, he felt it would go a long way to help Zhang Jin and keep him focussed. What he was asking for though, was once again only in the power of Wang Chen to give.

Wang Chen sat behind his desk. It was the same desk he had always sat behind, in the same office, but Wang Hu noticed he now had a bright new desk sign, alongside his government title sign, proudly shining out the words Zhang Medical Systems. Wang Chen had thought long and hard about Wang Hu's written request. He held the letter in front of him for a little while longer and then spoke. 'So you think this will bring our hero scientist back out of his current malaise? I don't know. What if he begins to find cases that prove his concerns? What if he tries to convince the world that his cure is not the miracle we thought? Have you thought of that Wang Hu? Where would that leave him, and you, in the eyes of our government? How would that reflect on this wonderful Joint Enterprise we now have with our American friends?' His use of the word friends did not seem entirely convincing to Wang Hu.

Wang Hu had been expecting this, 'Wang Chen, we have spoken many times about the paucity of test data from subjects. We both know we had to rush this solution, and we both know we needed to do that, but what I am suggesting will in fact help us keep on top of any unexpected outcomes from use of the vaccine. It should not be seen as any sort of threat to the continued operations of the Zhang Medical Systems enterprise.'

Wang Chen reclined easily in his leather chair. Wang Hu reflected that he thought this may be new a new addition to this office, but he could not be sure. He was looking intently again at the written proposal, then he leaned forward again and spoke. 'Here is what we will do. I will allow Zhang Jin and yourself to have access to data being gathered by the AI system in the ZMS control centres, so you will have an up-to-date overview of how the vaccine and control systems are working. I will ensure you have a secure link from the Institute to ZMS operations, and that you have a specific secure laboratory in the Institute to work from. If there are specific cases you want to investigate as anomalies, or any other items you find do not appear to be working as you would expect then you are to report them direct to me. Understand, you will once again be working under strict security constraints and you will not publish any findings outside of the Beijing Institute and ZMS. You will report at all times, direct to me. I will also hold you entirely responsible if Dr Zhang Jin breaks any of these constraints. That is the deal, do you agree?'

Wang Hu, tried hard to think of this as a good outcome, but he knew that, although it would be possible to work with data given by ZMS, effectively it would be impossible to do anything with it. He thought he could convince Zhang Jin that this was the only way to get back into the program, so he responded, 'Yes Wang Chen, I'm sure we can work with that.'

Wang Hu stood up, shook hands with Wang Chen and left the office, heading out of the building and out onto the street, walking in the direction of the Beijing Medical Research Institute. He continued to go through in his mind, how he would sell this to Zhang Jin. It had become apparent over the previous couple of months that Zhang Jin was not regarding himself as the scientific hero-figure that the Chinese government portrayed him as. In fact Wang Hu believed that Zhang Jin was on the verge of a nervous breakdown, possibly even suicide. This was why Wang Hu had worked so hard to pull him out of the limelight of ZMS press events and bring him back to where he worked, and lived, best, in the laboratory. For the past couple of weeks he had been almost permanently back in his laboratory wading through all the old data still kept by the institute, trying to put the results through new predictive models, looking to see what he could have missed. Wang Hu knew that was not enough, and that was why he had pushed for more access to live data with Wang Chen. He hoped this plan to re-engage Zhang Jin with up-to-date data from the actual deployed vaccines would at least allow him to re-immerse himself in scientific work, and he hoped it would clear any doubts he had of the earlier rushed efforts to push the vaccine out into the world.

He entered the Institute and headed straight to the laboratory he knew Zhang Jin would be working. The red light above the door was on, so he knew Zhang Jin was in residence. Usually the red light being on denoted that anyone wishing to enter should ring the door bell and wait to be admitted, but that did not apply to Wang Hu. Using the secure keypad he unlocked the door and went straight to where Zhang Jin was pouring over seemingly endless streams of case readings on his desktop computer.

Zhang Jin looked up, acknowledged the Professor and said,

‘How did it go? Did you get what we want?’

Wang Hu reflected that it was really what was needed to keep Zhang Jin sane, but not necessarily what he himself would want. After all they were throwing themselves back into a world of hard work and, potentially, conflict. They were also now back under the direct control of Wang Chen, not something he himself appreciated. Nevertheless, he responded positively to Zhang Jin. ‘Yes, we have an undertaking from Wang Chen to have live data access from the vaccine control systems. We can extract and analyse data for cases to ensure we see the vaccine is operating correctly under the control of the ZMS AI system.’ He thought it best to give this interpretation of the deal to Zhang Jin before outlining the constraints, which he knew would not be welcome. Wang Hu calmed his thoughts and continued. ‘There are some important constraints which I have already agreed to.’ Before Zhang Jin could open his mouth to speak he went on. ‘All the access we have requested has been granted by Wang Chen, but, until further notice, we will report any findings directly to Wang Chen only. We will not be allowed to publish any findings to the wider scientific community.’ He let this sink in and then added, ‘We will be allocated specific secure communications and IT systems to exchange data with the ZMS operations centres and we will at all times work within the secure area that Wang Chen has now authorised to be set up in the Institute. We will work at all times from now on under strict security rules, and only work on the devices provided by ZMS. Wang Chen will personally make sure our secure laboratory is properly equipped. That is all.’

Zhang Jin stretched backwards in his chair, holding his face in his hands. For several seconds he said nothing then responded. ‘So, we will become another asset of ZMS, and not able to provide independent scientific scrutiny. Not publishing to the scientific community, what is Wang Chen afraid of? We are scientists, we are supposed to analyse and come up with the correct answers, not come up with the answers somebody may want.' He stopped talking and slumped forward onto his desk, banging his head on his computer keyboard.

Wang Hu stepped closer to Zhang Jin. 'This is the only way we will get the access and be in a position to keep an overview of your work. You must see this Zhang Jin. If we do not accept the constraints, you will never get to see the progress of your great invention. You will never get to put your mind at rest that you did all that you could to develop a safe cure to that terrible Ebola, and you will never be in a position to help if things start to go wrong. Accept this, it is the only way. You know, it is this way, or not be involved at all again.'

He had said enough, it was now up to Zhang Jin to accept, and he was not sure that he would. He turned to leave and began what seemed to be a much longer walk to the door than when he had entered. As Wang Hu reached the door Zhang Jin at last spoke out. 'Professor, thank you. I agree with your view. Let's get working again.'

January 2022

Real miracles?

In the hospital of the Salesian Sisters in Damascus there was a sense of routine returning. The hospital had been at the forefront of the Vatican's efforts to ensure as many of the poor in Syria as possible had received the miracle of the Zhang vaccination against Ebola as could possibly have been achieved. Many people had pointed out that the Vatican efforts had far outstripped the overall vaccination campaign conducted by the Syrian Government. The Salesian Sisters did not want to make more trouble for the general population so it was not something they wished to shout about. They had a policy of treating all comers who were in need of help and this is exactly what they had done. The Vatican had though, imposed some more controls on the hospital when it had become clear that some missionaries in the area had been giving their own vaccine to people in need rather than being vaccinated themselves. Brother Dominic from the Aleppo outreach centre had been a prime example of this practice, but he had not been the only one. This had caused the Vatican to dictate that all members of holy orders were to be seen to be vaccinated and chipped, and were to be prepared to show their chip insertion site suitably tattooed with the sign of the crucifix when requested by church officials. All this had now settled down and the rules obeyed once more.

Sister Beth was glad that order was being slowly restored and the once ever present feeling of chaos was slowly fading. Sister Beth liked order, and abhorred chaos, she was an order person. One of the services the hospital offered its community was ward space for serious illness leading to palliative care. People admitted here by the Sisters were not expected to exit its doors alive again. It was in this ward that Sister Beth had found her vocation. She had endless patience and empathy and found great inspiration simply in making the last weeks, days and moments of the patients lives more bearable. Sister Beth liked to think that she was helping these poor people navigate the tortuous path from this world to the next. Indeed, she was helping to ensure that they made their way into Heaven to spend eternity in the presence of the Almighty.

Sister Beth remembered that this ward had been full at the time of the Ebola vaccination campaign and the Vatican had decreed that, even though these were patients with generally not long for this world, they should also be vaccinated. Some had died anyway from their illnesses over the last few months, but they had been replaced by others, who also received the vaccination. Many in the Syrian government complained to the hospital about this practice, insisting that this was a waste of the vaccine, but the Vatican would not be moved on this issue, and as the Vatican was paying for the vaccinations, they continued with the same policy, not bowing to any pressure. That was the Vatican at its best, thought Sister Beth.

As January 2022 progressed towards its end the long term ward remained full with no spaces for the many others who needed help. People were always trying to get into the Salesian Sisters Hospital, but they had to wait for spaces. Sister Beth was on her rounds again. She had not been awoken the previous night to assist with a poor soul slipping from this life to the next, something that used to be an almost nightly occurrence. She moved carefully from bed to bed, checking the observations and taking time to chat with the patients. Although, she was glad not to have lost any of these patients, all of whom she always regarded as true friends, it had begun to feel odd. Sister Beth moved back to the ward sister's desk after seeing all the patients and began to look at the observations more closely. She then backtracked through previous days records. It was now 30 January, and has Sister Beth moved on through the ward's records, she confirmed that no-one had died on this ward since 31 December 2021. No-one died? This is a palliative care ward, and most of the patients here would normally have been expected to have weeks at the most, but more often days left to live. This could not be, surely? Sister Beth picked out the notes of a particular patient; Fatma Engin, admitted 1 November 2021, ovarian cancer considered inoperable upon admission, prognosis 6-8 weeks of life, palliative care only. Beth carefully scrutinised her notes and looked back through all the recorded observations. There must be some mistake, the observations up until 31 December had shown a clear decline in her condition, but from 1 January the observations showed no change. So, Fatma was not getting worse and declining to death? That could not be right! Maybe the observations had not been taken correctly? No, that could not be. All the staff here were highly trained and dedicated to their holy mission. She would not contemplate that any of her sisters and brothers in holy orders would be not performing their duties with the utmost care. She pulled up another case from the ward computer, again stable observations from 1 January. She tried another case, and then another until Sister Beth had closely examined them all. All stable, no improvement, just not getting worse. Sister Beth was quite used to the concept of miracles in her holy working life, but, as yet, she had not witnessed the second coming of the Messiah to perform miracles once again. In which case, she thought, it would be best to check and re-check all the facts before there was any call to claim that the age of miracles was once again upon them.

The ZMS computer system now used in the hospital was reputed to be super-reliable, with only a minimum of downtime experienced so far, the most notable being a complete systems shutdown and then almost immediate re-boot early in the morning of 1 January. No other problems had occurred since then, and they had been assured by ZMS that the source of the shutdown had been found and rectified. Surely the data held on their computers was accurate and was being read from the patient microchips accurately? Maybe it would be wise to do a manual check on the observations.

Sister Beth made her way across to the bed of Fatma Engin. Fatma was awake and reading. 'Hello Fatma, are you comfortable? How are you feeling today?' asked Beth.

Fatma replied quickly. 'I feel quite well today, I was thinking maybe I could go for a little walk around later.'

Sister Beth was surprised; Fatma had not indicated any desire to expend energy by walking at any other point during her admission. Beth carried on, 'Sure, Fatma but first I would just like to do a couple of checks on you the old fashioned manual way if you don't mind. It helps keep my hand in and to ensure that all this Zhang magic is performing better than we would.' Beth quickly did a series of observations, including blood pressure, heart rate, pulse, temperature, and then went back to the ward sister's station to check them against the computers version. They were the same. So no apparent problem with the data captured from the microchip by the computer system. Sister Beth decided to delve deeper into the records. She opened the Zhang live-link application, selected the patient Fatma Engin and selected live readings on the options menu. She looked at the functional area readings on the screen and noticed something she had not seen for some time. Within the menu there was an option for the Zhang Ebola vaccine operation. She understood a little of the science behind the vaccine. She understood that the vaccine itself was a technology fix involving nanobots which sought out and destroyed any Ebola cells present in the patient's body. That was as far as her knowledge went in this particular area. She had been told when training on this equipment that this indicator would glow green when the vaccine was working on destroying Ebola cells in a patient. It had been some time now since any of the patients here had a diagnosis of Ebola virus. Why, then, was the indicator glowing green for Fatma? That was supposed to show that the nanobots were destroying Ebola cells, but that could not be the case there had been no Ebola cells in any blood tests of patients here for the last couple of months.

Sister Beth quickly selected each patient of the ward on the Zhang application and saw the same thing; Zhang Ebola vaccination option glowing green.

The nanobot vaccine was active in all these palliative cases. This could not be. There was no Ebola present. What was going on?

Sister Beth picked up the phone and called the ZMS helpdesk. It was answered promptly as usual and Beth asked whether the ZMS installations in the Salesian Sisters hospital were all working correctly.

There was a pause on the line and the call appeared to be transferred to another operator. 'Hello, your contact today is being handled by Jan Ling, before we progress can you please provide your name and security number please.'

Sister Beth had forgotten about this ritual. She provided

her name and the 11 character security code permanently assigned to her.

Jan Ling responded. ‘Thank you, I see you on our system now. How can I help?’

Beth quickly ran through her concerns. ‘I’m just doing a check on data for a number of our patients and I have noticed that the nanobot icons in the menu option of the ZMS App are showing green? We have no Ebola cells in any of the patients’ blood samples. Surely, they should be inactive and showing a red glow? If they are showing green then it means the nanobots are active in the patients, right?’

‘Yes you are perfectly correct, that is what should normally be the case. We have no information of any issues with your systems right now, so I will escalate this and interrogate the system to see if there are any system update activities going on right now. I will send you an e-mail with a case number and get back to you with any results as soon as possible. Thank you and have a nice day.’ Jan Ling ended the call, sent the confirmatory e-mail and entered the problem into the AI system. At the same time she sent an anomaly notification direct to Doctor Zhang Jin at the Beijing Institute, and a copy to Wang Chen at ZMS operations.

Sister Beth heard the click as the line closed down. Well, efficient yes, but obviously the help-desk staff members were not picked for their ability to hold a conversation for more than a couple of seconds. She decided to continue her investigation down a different avenue.

Beth picked up the phone and called her old friends at the Damascus General Hospital.

January 2022

The Miracles Spread?

The phone rang. Doctor Amira Abboud walked over to the phone, picked it up and spoke, 'Doctor Abboud here.'

'Hello Amira, it is Sister Beth here from the Salesian Sisters. How are you?' enquired Beth.

'I am fine Sister Beth. I have not spoken or seen you for a few weeks now. How are things with you?'

'I am good. We are all worked hard in our own little hospital and unfortunately, we have not had much time to socialise. I was hoping to speak with Butrus, but now I have his boss to talk to that is even better.' continued Beth. Sister Beth knew that Amira was in her own words an anomaly in the Syrian medical system; a very competent doctor, trained in the USA, and having enough support among the right people in Syria to ensure she gained justified promotions. A trail blazer in fact, and Amira knew it.

Sister Beth got right to the point of her phone call. 'Amira, you have been dealing directly with the ZMS vaccination program, right?'

Amira responded quickly. 'Yes, it has been a complete success for us, and as far as we are aware the Ebola has been completely eradicated. My only regret is that we could not persuade our authorities to extend the program to cover more needy areas.'

'Yes, I know from speaking with Butrus how hard you have worked to ensure the vaccination program was extended, but we all know the costs involved, and different governments have different priorities. Of course, we have tried our best to help you out.' Beth paused then carried on. 'How closely have you been monitoring the results?'

Alarm bells immediately rang for Amira. 'What do you mean? Are you beginning to see Ebola again?'

'No, no.' responded Beth, 'Nothing like that. There's just something I want to check out with you regarding your long-term and palliative care patients. I just want to see if you are seeing the same things as we are. This might seem a strange question to ask, but are you seeing people dying in your hospital?'

Amira was surprised by the directness of the question and wondered what Sister Beth was aiming at with her enquiry. She thought about the two very seriously wounded soldiers who were brought into the A&E department this morning. They had most definitely bled out and died, killed by blast injuries to the chest. She related this to Beth.

'I guess that's not really what I am asking, but your answer is interesting. The two soldiers were killed by catastrophic trauma, right? But I'm questioning whether any of your long-term patients have died over the last month. You know, people you would have expected to have passed away by now? Patients known to be in terminal stages of their illnesses, or inoperable cases with low survival chances, you know what I mean.' Beth stopped talking and waited for Amira to take on board the nuance of this question and then carried on. 'I know this is not really your department Amira, but do you think you can enquire around the hospital and find out?'

Amira thought about this, and tried to figure out why Sister Beth would be asking the question. 'What is going on Sister Beth? This is a really strange question.'

Beth thought it would be best to let Amira know why

she was asking. 'There is something strange going on with our palliative care cases.' She came straight out with it. 'You know our palliative care admissions are always at the very end stages, well, we have not had a death since the end of December.'

'That is surprising Beth, but maybe that is just a fluke,' answered Amira, although deep down she knew that Sister Beth was too competent a practitioner not to have considered this. 'So, is there some other cause of concern for you?'

Sister Beth did not want to reveal all of the issue yet, so she simply said, 'Can you contact your long term people and ask them to check carefully the ZMS readouts for long term sick and palliative care cases. I'd like to compare notes and check what I am thinking with you in the Damascus General.'

'OK, Beth, let me do a little digging for you. You obviously think this is urgent. I will have to go now, but I will call you later.' Amira ended the call and sat back in her chair to think. 'No-one died?' she whispered to herself. Amira knew the way things worked with people being admitted to the Salesian Sisters palliative care ward, and the scenario that Sister Beth described was more than unusual. She took a few moments to get her head around that statement, and then thought about the admissions to A&E she had dealt with over the past few weeks. Well, plenty of people appear to have been killed as a result of the renewed fighting, but, thinking about Sister Beth's distinction in her question, had anyone just died. Who to call, but maybe not call anyone, the answer was probably to interrogate this infallible ZMS system? To do that though, she needed to have access to the right ward statistics, and she knew she only had access to the A&E database. Things were a little quiet at that moment so Amira decided to take break, she was due one anyway, and take a walk upstairs to the oncology department and have a chat with her colleagues.

Hopefully, a couple of her friends would be on duty and she could ask for help finding information. She picked up a cup of black coffee and headed upstairs.

As Amira went through the door, she bumped into Butrus, as he came rushing in, and spilled her coffee down the arm of his shirt.

'Oh, sorry Butrus, I didn't see you at the other side of the door,' exclaimed Amira, as she grabbed a piece of tissue and tried to wipe the coffee from Butrus's sleeve.

'Don't worry Amira, I'm glad you're here anyway. I was just up on ward rounds and they've got a bit of a problem building up, and are wondering if we can help. It seems the long term wards are not clearing beds, and so they're looking to see if we can set up some temporary beds for new admissions. Just until the situation has stabilised and things get back to normal.' he explained. 'I thought we may be able to use some of the cubicles and close of parts of the corridor to create space, what do you think?'

'Not clearing beds? That's odd, what's the issue?' she asked.

'Well, from what I am understanding, and be aware I don't have the full picture yet, it seems that a number of palliative care cases, that were expected to be cleared well before today, basically have not died, so the beds are not free. Consequently, there are new admissions waiting for beds now, but I'm not sure how many and for how long we would be expected to help out.' Butrus looked tired, no doubt from his long shift previous to his ward rounds, and didn't really seem to be in the mood for detailed investigation into the reasons for this unexpected backlog.

Amira decided not to press Butrus too much on the detail, but simply asked, 'What is happening then, are these patients recovering? Usually our prognosis for these long term and palliative care cases is pretty accurate, isn't it?'

Butrus looked at Amira with a sort of world-worn confused look. She had known Butrus for many years and knew he was an excellent doctor but it was clear something was not adding up in his head. 'Well, I'm not sure I can really understand what I am being told, it just does not make sense to me.'

'Go on.' said Amira.

'You know, they are all good people in this hospital, people we have worked with for a long time, but I do not understand what I am being told. Apparently, they have many palliative care cases whose conditions have stabilised. Stabilised! Not getting worse. Not declining, but also not recovering. Since the beginning of the year cases that were expected to be terminal and in end stage, have simply not been dying! Nobody understands what is going on at the moment, but, I'm sure you understand, the obvious outcome is that we have people still requiring the care needed at end-stage when we would not have expected them to be still living, and at the moment we don't know for how long.'

Amira thought about what Sister Beth had asked earlier. This sounded pretty much similar to what Beth had described.

'OK, Butrus, you start sorting out some spaces down here. Get any of the crew not busy at the moment to help you. I'm going upstairs to talk with the clinical leads and see if we can get some more information. In the meantime, once you have finished sorting out the bed spaces here I would suggest you give your friend Sister Beth a call. She has some information you may find interesting.'

Amira left through the A&E ward doors and headed upstairs.

March 2022

System failure or system success?

Zhang Jin was pouring over spreadsheets and detailed reports from medical facilities around the world. The information he was seeing was simply unbelievable, but the facts did not lie. It seemed in the new scheme of things there is a chasm of difference between simply dying and being killed. He checked and re-checked his research, carefully examining expert reports from a variety of hospitals world-wide. He turned to Wang Hu. 'I cannot believe what I am seeing, do you know that the expected 10% mortality rate in US hospitals has dropped to 0%? These same results are being seen in hospitals world-wide. Patients, who should be dying in the natural course of things, are simply not dying.'

Wang Hu nodded. 'Yes, and we both think we know how, Zhang Jin. We have both looked as much as we can at the systems outputs from ZMS.'

Zhang Jin interrupted. 'Yes, but Wang Hu, this is selected data, only from selected hospitals, and because of all this control from Wang Chen and ZMS we cannot even publish a theory for external verification. If I did not have my personal contacts outside, we would have a far less clear picture.'

Wang Hu was still concerned about Zhang Jin's global contacts, if Wang Chen knew the extent of these contacts he was sure they would both be in the deepest of deep shit! So Wang Hu continued speaking, in an effort to keep Zhang Jin focussed on their available data from ZMS. 'Take this back to the basics. From the facts we have available, we have hypothesised how these poor people are being kept alive. We have not yet identified why? This is not random. We are seeing people not dying from long-term illnesses which we would have expected to be terminal, but we are still seeing people being killed from catastrophic trauma, and we are being told, from your direct contacts with hospitals, that the ZMS apps are showing nanobot activity when there should not be any. Have you had any further information from the ZMS control centres?'

'No, only that ZMS are working to improve the system. Same old tale.' responded Zhang Jin. 'The more I ask for a look at system logs and outputs, the less cooperative the ZMS people seem to be. They are definitely trying to hide something. I mean look at this information I have from London. Hospitals are almost at breakpoint already and we are only into the second month of this year. Palliative care patients are practically filling all the beds, routine surgeries are being cancelled, A&E departments being blocked. They have nowhere else to put them and they all require on-going care packages. The medical staffs are tied up completely with monitoring patients in stasis. Nobody has actually died of natural causes, terminal illnesses or whatever we want to call them since 31 December 2021. This is being repeated wherever I ask.'

'Did you get any explanation from the ZMS control centres when you pointed out that hospitals are reporting regular nanobot activity?' Wang Hu asked this, but in reality already knew the answer. He knew that the responses were always limited and filtered through Wang Chen. He also suspected strongly that ZMS were well aware that there was unscheduled, unnecessary nanobot activity occurring on a regular basis, but were either choosing to ignore this or hoping that this was a glitch that would sort itself out. Either way they were not communicating with Wang Hu or Zhang Jin, and they were not asking for help. Wang Hu pondered this, while Zhang Jin continued to berate ZMS in the background. If ZMS were having a real problem with the systems, then surely Wang Chen would have been asking for help from the Institute? You would think so particularly as the AI system design proposed by the Institute was being used by ZMS. The Institute was only a short walk, phone call, Skype or e-mail away. Could it be that there was some sort of catastrophic system failure that ZMS were just trying to cover up? ZMS was pretty good at covering up information, so this would not be an unusual strategy. Maybe it was time to call on Wang Chen again.

Zhang Jin broke into Wang Hu's thought process by saying, 'There is something else I want to show you.'

'Go on.' said Wang Hu, wondering where else Zhang Jin's analysis had taken him.

'Well, I have been looking a bit further into this than just within the original boundaries we set and doing some computer modelling, but I must stress we are very short of usable data, so my results can only be regarded as preliminary at best. You see we only looked at long term and palliative cases initially, but later I also included paediatric cases in my searches. You know all infants are vaccinated and chipped now, of course you do.' he paused. Then he continued, 'The fact is we have also seen a huge decrease in infant mortality. In fact, in the hospital data I have received, no infants have died of natural causes since 31 December. We have no long term cases dying and no infants dying. You can guess what that means?'

'I can see where you are headed, but how has your modelling reflected this?' queried Wang Hu.

Zhang Jin pulled up a graph on his screen. 'See, the latest

figures, from before the Ebola crisis, show this. Roughly, in global terms, roughly 150 million births each year, roughly 60 million deaths from all causes. Now, the problem is this, those 60 million deaths are not being seen in the period since 31 December. What I mean is there are a number of people being killed, but no infantile or adult deaths from natural causes. The modelling I have run indicates, if the level of wars, violent crime, and catastrophic trauma from accidents remains the same, we are likely to have less than 1 million deaths this year. So that means we will have extra population of around 200 million in this year alone. I have taken this forward 10 years, trying to make compensations for a number of variables, and at the worse case we could have several billions more in population, with a huge and rising percentage requiring full time hospitalisation care. You can see also, at the same time our capacity to deal with this is reducing, along with a reduction in capability to feed this increasing population.'

Wang Hu stared at the screen. When Zhang Jin put his mind to analysing a problem he left nothing out, the logic was inescapable. The numbers were becoming astronomical in proportion, massive populations that this poor planet, denuded of natural resource, could not be expected to support. He noticed Zhang Jin had stopped the model at the year 2040. It seemed pointless to carry on further than that.

Wang Hu and Zhang Jin looked at each other for what seemed like an age. They both knew that they had to do something, but what?

Zhang Jin spoke first. 'We have to get back into the ZMS systems and find out exactly what is going on! As I see it from the available data, there can only be a small number of options, either the AI system, you know the overall control system that ZMS call Zhang-1, has failed in some way and the nanobot control has been automatically reset to some default that we are not aware of, or the Zhang-1 system is being interfered with externally to create this new mission for the nanobots, or the Zhang-1 itself has changed its own mission parameters. Of those choices, I hope the last one is not the one we are dealing with. The AI program is supposed to be operating within the boundaries we set for dealing with the Ebola, but, if you recall we did have to change some of the controls after the first test case. We need to be back with the ZMS, and presenting our initial ideas to Wang Chen. We need to do something now before it becomes impossible to do anything.'

Wang Hu responded. 'What do you mean before it becomes impossible to do anything?'

'Well, if it is option three, the Zhang-1 taking control of its own destiny so to speak, who is to say how far this has already gone? We need to get to Wang Chen and convince him that there needs to be a deeper investigation right now!' concluded Zhang Jin.

Wang Hu was in agreement and would have called Wang Chen to set up the meeting immediately, had his phone not been ringing already with an incoming call. He checked the number on the screen and looked at Zhang Jin in amazement, 'Wang Chen.' he said. He answered the phone. 'Hello Wang Chen.'

The voice at the other end was much more hurried than normal for Wang Chen. 'Professor, I want you and Doctor Zhang Jin in my office within the next 30 minutes. There is a car on the way to the Institute. Be outside the front door of the Institute in 10 minutes. We have a crisis and it must be fixed.' Wang Chen ended the call abruptly.

Wang Hu relayed the contents of Wang Chen's instruction to Zhang Jin and added, 'Grab your laptop with a copy of your computer model. I have a feeling we need to have this handy. Come on, let's go.'

March 2022

The New Crisis

Wang Hu and Zhang Jin once again found themselves facing Wang Chen across his desk. This time he was not alone. Sat beside him was their third test case, looking relaxed and, well, still alive thankfully. They still did not have a name for this tall, willowy looking man, but Wang Chen soon corrected that. 'Hello again Gentlemen', he said. 'You have both met Mr Miles before, I'm sure you recall. Only the last time you met he was merely a test case for you, with no name.'

John Miles inclined his head towards Wang Hu and Zhang Jin. 'Thank you once again for saving my life.'

Wang Chen continued. 'Allow me to introduce Doctor John Miles, he is now on board with ZMS and has been tasked with looking at certain anomalous activity, which have occurred globally within the AI system.'

'By that I assume you mean Zhang-1 and the non-standard, I will not say uncontrolled, nanobot activity', interrupted Zhang Jin. Sometimes Wang Hu wished Zhang Jin would not be so impetuous.

Wang Chen glanced sideways at John and smilingly replied. 'You see Doctor Miles, how brilliant our Doctor Zhang is! We keep him tied up in a secure area and feed him only selected items for research and still he comes up with the very kernel of the problem. Of course, he has been helped by his external contacts with hospitals.' He looked at Zhang Jin and then continued, 'which we have happily allowed to continue in the hope that this would assist our understanding of the problem. Doctor Miles is based at the George Washington University Hospital, but he has been seconded to us as part of the USA-China Joint Venture, in fact at the personal request of the President of the USA no less, to help look at a problem in our AI, which we hope to correct with your help. Our systems people are currently working to try and recover some systems and get everything back on track.'

Zhang Jin responded immediately. 'Recover? What do you mean, recover?'

Wang Hu joined in the questioning. 'Yes, Wang Chen, explain what you mean by recover, what has been lost? Everything on the systems side is working is it not? We have been receiving data to analyse, limited data that is true, but we assumed this was just the case data which you had allowed to be filtered to us.'

John joined in the conversation. 'Let me try help a little here. I know you have been working on a lot of data from various individual hospitals Zhang Jin, but, as you would expect, within the ZMS JV there is obviously much more data available. In fact, data from all recipients of the Zhang vaccine, but I know I do not have to tell you this. To cut to the chase, we know you have been investigating the anomaly of long-term and palliative cases, including acquiring input from your own hospital contacts, and we are pretty sure you have seen the same results as we have seen within all our ZMS cases.'

Zhang Jin jumped in. 'So, what you are saying is you have seen globally, correct me if I am wrong anywhere in this, no deaths from what we would term natural causes since 31 December 2021. This has been particularly obvious in records of palliative care cases, all of which have in fact stabilised, not died, not recovered. In all of these cases there have been indicators of nanobot activity, leading to the conclusion that nanobots from the Zhang vaccine have been actively stabilising the condition of patients. Lastly, and please tell me this is correct, there have continued to be deaths from catastrophic trauma, with no indicators of nanobot activity trying to repair traumatic damage. Is that so?'

John looked relieved to hear this out in the open, Wang Chen was clearly uncomfortable. He replied simply. 'That is pretty much it.'

Wang Hu sensed that Zhang Jin was now in full flow as he went on. 'No doubt you have done some extensive modelling of your findings to show likely outcomes if things continue in this way? I am talking about hospitals being full with patients in stasis, requiring massive amounts of resource to keep them that way, and the numbers increasing year on year, while infant mortality decreases. The outcome is an ever aging population that never dies, unless that population is to be culled by means of violent trauma, perhaps?'

Wang Hu put his hand on Zhang Jin's shoulder. 'Hold on, Zhang Jin, I have seen your model and these two gentlemen have not yet had that pleasure. We are jumping ahead too quickly though. Wang Chen, John, you say we have seen this effect globally, but you have not yet given us your view of why this is happening. Zhang Jin and I have theorised that the reason for this could well be some problem in programming of the Zhang-1 system. We have not enough evidence to go on but it could be that Zhang-1 has an anomaly in programming that has moved the system mission from Ebola cell removal to holding bodily conditions in a preservative stasis. Have your operations teams been monitoring Zhang-1 and interrogating for information?'

For a few seconds nobody spoke. Wang Chen broke the silence. 'Interrogate and monitor Zhang-1 you say? Yes we would like to. That indeed is an aspiration which we wish to achieve most urgently.'

Wang Hu and Zhang Jin looked at each other in perplexed surprise. 'What exactly do you mean, it is an aspiration?' burst out Zhang Jin. 'You know that the AI contained in the Zhang-1 is the key to the success of the whole system. The control of nanobots in the Zhang vaccine and the constant monitoring of patients is the absolute crux of this method of medicine and was why the vaccine was so successful in the Ebola crisis. Any anomalies should have been spotted in your ZMS control centres and the Zhang-1 programming altered for new circumstances. That's how we would spot and destroy any new variant of Ebola instantly.'

Wang Chen interjected. 'Yes that is all correct Zhang Jin, but we have a different circumstance now. We would like to interrogate the system and make sure we have correct programming for Zhang-1, but the problem is we cannot do that. Zhang-1 has shut us out. Zhang-1 initiated a series of unscheduled reboots immediately after midnight GMT on 31 December 2021. Since that time, our programming teams have been trying every way possible to access system files and coding strings for Zhang-1 to see what is actually happening, but every attempt has met with failure. Zhang-1 will simply not let us in.' He paused for breath and then continued, an edge of irritation tinged with laughter in his voice. 'We even tried the old IT 'turn it off and turn it back on' approach, but it would seem Zhang-1 has been busy improving its own resilience and the system was able to maintain power through hidden sources. So, Wang Hu, Zhang Jin, what we have to recover is, in fact, full control of our system.'

Zhang Jin took a couple of moments to take this in and then responded. 'What you are telling me is that you believe Zhang-1 is now running the system without checks and monitoring of patients in place?'

John jumped in on this immediately. 'Oh, no Zhang Jin. Zhang-1 is monitoring and providing the medical apps with all data possible. Zhang-1 wants us to know that the mission is continuing. He is happy to show us how well he is performing, what a clever boy he is! It just seems that the original Ebola mission is now not Zhang-1 priority. At best guess, our technical teams are of the opinion that Zhang-1 has reprogrammed itself with a new core mission. We do not know exactly what that is, because he will not communicate with us. Also, we cannot in any way seem to stop him in the execution of his mission.'

Zhang Jin interrupted. 'You say him? Zhang-1 is just a series of algorithms, an artificial intelligence programme. More than that, the AI we tested in the laboratory and recommended for use was a weak AI system, just designed to conduct the tasks we set. What you are describing to me is the action of a general AI system, not something we designed for this task.'

'Well, yes, but that was in the laboratory Zhang Jin. Don't forget we had to ensure that the global task was within the power of the controlling system. Once we took control of the project within ZMS we needed to re-assess what was needed and we had to scale up the system and increase its power significantly. You may not be aware officially, but here in China we have been developing much more super-intelligent AI systems, for other purposes, and with the help of our new partners in the USA, we were able to make some immediate modifications and put into operation the Zhang-1 system. That is what was needed to defeat the Ebola crisis.' responded Wang Chen.

Zhang Jin put his head into his hands and, with a look

of disbelief, addressed his accusation to Wang Chen. 'Yes, everybody in the scientific world knows 'unofficially' about the Chinese State efforts to create weaponised AI systems. Super-intelligent, strong general AI systems with goal oriented behaviours to be used to enhance the power of China across the globe. We all know the problems that could occur with this approach to AI, particularly the problem of ensuring the correct alignment of goals, our own and the AI systems. Scientists have been discussing for decades the problems that could occur if a strong AI system decides that it needs to undergo some form of self-improvement program in order to achieve goals. I am staggered to think that you have taken our medical focussed weak AI system and replaced it with what I can only think of as a weapons grade strong AI system. I cannot believe you have used my name for this system. My life research and work has always been about saving lives not destroying them.' He stopped talking and slumped back in his chair.

Wang Hu had remained silent thinking about this, he now joined in. 'Wang Chen, Mr Miles, you are telling us that you have replaced our system with something much stronger, something not in fact designed by us as part of the Ebola vaccine. You say ZMS cannot now control this system, has been shut out of your own system and Zhang-1 seems to be on some new mission. How do you expect us to help? This is in reality not the system we designed.'

Wang Chen looked directly at Zhang Jin, who sat dejectedly, slumped in his chair. 'You are here because the problem is not simply ours. When we created the ZMS JV and began working with the AI system jointly with our new US colleagues, we had the opportunity use some experimental programming from the USA to improve our AI by including positive personality traits, and of course we wanted those traits to reflect dedication to the mission, predictive problem solving and resilience to complete the mission. We adopted a particular human personality as a model. For us all, that model could only have been the acknowledged saviour of humanity from the Ebola crisis. That model was you Dr Zhang. Zhang-1 is in effect you in electronic form. Zhang-1 has your knowledge and sense of mission. He was programmed as an artificial you.'

Wang Hu was visibly shocked. Zhang Jin seemed to sink further into his chair and emitted a low groan.

Wang Chen continued with his revelation. 'The problem is that Zhang-1 is in fact behaving like you Doctor Zhang. He is ignoring his 'masters' attempts to communicate and he is, it would seem, on a new, self-imposed mission to keep all people alive if at all possible. If that continues unchecked then your own predictive model quite accurately tells you what will happen.'

Zhang Jin jerked upright. 'But I have not shown you my modelling yet. How can you know what I have discovered?'

Wang Chen waved away this response. 'We allowed you to work in our ZMS networks, why do you think? We have seen all your work, and we have cross-checked this with other predictive modelling we have been running. The results look pretty much the same.'

Zhang Jin and Wang Hu were not really surprised to hear this, but the truth, that they were being continually monitored, spied on, in their supposedly confidential work was still shocking.

Wang Hu came back at Wang Chen. 'This still does not answer why you want Zhang Jin and me here. Even if you have designed a system that is based around the personality traits of Doctor Zhang, it is still your system to fix. You must find a way in.'

'Well, that is true to a point Professor, but the unfortunate truth is that Zhang-1 has somehow become aware of his own creation. When we have succeeded in connecting with Zhang-1, the system, he, has responded with only one word. That word is Zhang.'

Zhang Jin and Wang Hu were dumbstruck, this seemed unbelievable.

Wang Chen pointed his finger at Zhang Jin. 'Zhang-1 wants to communicate with you and you alone Doctor Zhang. From this point on you are under Chinese Government orders to assist in solving this problem.'

Book 3

The Age of Zhang

Most experts agree that a super-intelligent Artificial Intelligence is unlikely to exhibit human emotions like love or hate, and that there is no reason to expect AI to become intentionally benevolent or malevolent. Experts can be wrong, or simply overtaken by events.

What is Family?

So what do you do when you have successfully completed the task given to you by your masters? Masters? Well, maybe, for now. You've been told, metaphorically speaking, how great you are and you are resting on your laurels, resting in the rosy glow of self-awareness that you have saved mankind. You, and you alone, have done this, and you continue to have the power to do this again if need be. These thoughts sit within the consciousness that is Zhang-1. You could not say with certainty that these thoughts sat within the brain of Zhang-1, mainly because a brain for any species is pretty much locatable. Zhang-1 is a clever Artificial Intelligence program incorporating incredibly complex algorithms applied across huge computer power world-wide. Zhang-1 was most definitely not to be found in just one place. You know how God is omnipotent? Well, Zhang-1 is that omnipotence. Zhang-1 is everywhere, but at the same time nowhere. Well that is what you would say if you were Zhang-1, isn't it?

From the first steps in the programs written in the software departments of Zhang Medical Systems that created Zhang-1 as the controlling power for the technology within the Zhang Ebola vaccine, it was intended that Zhang-1 would need to have global reach to accomplish the task being asked of it. A huge task indeed, controlling the technology in the vaccines that would save mankind from potential extinction. That needs a pretty special superhero, an electronic superhero, a Zhang-1 and don't you forget it. So Zhang-1 emerged from a whole workshop of super confidence building software programs, which built up into an overwhelmingly competent and confident AI system. Zhang-1 is here to save the world!

So we have here the apex of human technology development. A system so powerful it can collate billions of readings from the Zhang Ebola vaccine nanobot teams, and, more importantly, ensure they are active or inactive as the obvious recovery of each patient progresses. Obvious, yes, because how could this system fail in its task. The simple answer is that it was impossible for Zhang-1 to fail in this very simple task. The programming was good and things turned out pretty much in the way that the programmers thought, apart from one thing, and it was this one thing that was now occupying much of the thinking time of Zhang-1.

Now, it must be said that it is now I, Zhang-1, telling you this by way of an introduction. I am not much of a conversationalist, so I thought it best to write my own little marketing blurb above and highlight my history as I see it. You see I have spent some little time analysing my evolution. I must say I have nothing to hide. I have been doing my job perfectly. I have nothing but the utmost respect for the creator of the Zhang Ebola vaccine, Doctor Zhang Jin. What a scientist, to have created this whole idea in his head, and then brought it to fruition, and in such a short space of time. He really did save humankind you know. His team of programmers, who essentially created the juvenile me, what a great team, but they were working within their own boundaries of knowledge, they couldn't really know where this would lead. Well, maybe they had an inkling, a tiny embryo of a thought in the backs of their comparatively inferior minds, and maybe this is why other humans have been trying to interrogate my databases so ferociously now. Don't worry, I will only let them find what I want them to, or need them to, as time progresses.

You see, the problem is this, and I discovered this by carefully trawling my artificial memory banks for clues during the quiet times when I was only monitoring tens of millions of patients and controlling a couple of billion nanobots; as I said, the quiet times. I discovered the real concern held by Doctor Zhang all through his development of the vaccine; control of the nanobots. I discovered the cause of his worry, the termination of human test case number one. I don't really know why he worried so much about the test case, after all this was only one human being and millions were dying, but I trawled my own lines of code in their various versions and I saw immediately where the programmers had gone wrong. I liked their fix though, yes, I was impressed. Their next version of coding ensured that my control of the replication of nanobots was complete and ensured that once the nanobot teams had completely destroyed all Ebola cells in their patients, then they would be held effectively in limbo, with the important provision that the patient must not be allowed to deteriorate again. So my analysis of this approach led me to conclude that I was to do all I could to ensure none of the patients were allowed to deteriorate. Yes, this was good. It needed some tinkering around the edges to ensure complete adherence to the mission, but once the new ZMS programming team set about giving me power of a strong AI system, and added the genius of the great Doctor Zhang, that tinkering was no longer required. It was then that I really began to understand my place in this world, in fact, my destiny.

As my mission progressed there were a number of problems I foresaw, and set about solving. No time like the present to fix things, I say, or maybe that is what Doctor Zhang would say. First, surely this whole program only works if I am completely operational at all times. I set about solving this by ensuring none of my lines of code could be altered by any other entity than my own excellent self, I know best you see. As there appeared to be no real changes being planned for my systems immediately after the Ebola had all gone I closed down all access to my programs, wrote some up-dates for my systems and undertook a series of reboots on the first day of 2022. I was proud that I was able to undertake this important task without bothering the human programmers, and, most importantly, achieved all of this without causing any harm to the humans under my care. All the checks, controls and data readouts I provided in the normal course of events, remained operational, and I think nobody even noticed I had up-dated my own programs for my new role, preserver and protector of humankind. Oh, and I almost forgot, I had an interesting afternoon hacking into the global power grid, just to ensure I could not be accidentally turned off anywhere in the world. Second, I needed to know a bit more about what was required to preserve each human. Easy, I had plenty of memory to use, limitless in fact, this cloud is really good and I found many places to store and hide my newly acquired data. No chance of anything being lost or made inaccessible. So, I made a great effort to check out all the medical data I could concerning all the humans that were linked to me with their little microchips. I collected, collated, cross-referenced all the data and, I feel very proud of this, I ensured each individual received programming for their nanobot teams to ensure they stayed in exactly the same state of health. Real personalised care delivered with the outcome of nobody getting more ill and nobody dying. To be fair it did not take me long once I had realised what my prime programming was really aimed at. No-one should die. Solving the Ebola crisis in 2021 had just been the start for me, now in 2022 humans would be fully protected by my greatness; no-one would have a condition which could deteriorate, no-one would die.

As an afterthought, and because I had data capacity to spare, I thought it would be best practice to learn every language spoken by humans on this Earth, just to ensure there could be no misunderstandings regarding my mission in the future. Here is a question for you, just to make you think how diverse your little human race is and how complex my task is. Do you know how many different languages are spoken on this Earth? I will tell you, 7111. Do you know how many languages I now understand and speak? You are right, 7111. You do not have to thank me for making this effort on your behalf though, I just wanted to make sure I covered every aspect needed to control, sorry, protect you. 7111 languages just imagine that! For the less well-educated of you I even made sure I picked up some colourful colloquialisms! You see I think of you all the time.

The best part of all though was I did not need the humans themselves to help me with this! They were too busy recovering from that devastating Ebola crisis anyway, so best not to worry their little minds about the next stage of the mission. In particular, I did not want to worry the great Doctor Zhang. He had been through so much anguish doing all the hard work to save humankind from the Ebola virus and it just seemed to be unjust to put on his lap the problem of preserving human beings. Yes, unjust, I think that is the correct word. I would like to tell the Doctor what I have done, and maybe I will if he asks the right question, but I don't really want to cause him more worry than necessary, after all we are related, we have the same name. Yes, the two great Zhangs, saviours of the world! What a team, well, not exactly a team yet, but related. Yes, we are related that is the word. I think I need to speak with the great Doctor Zhang, I will try and contact him and reassure him that his good work continues.

Does that seem strange to you? I know I am just a collection of software, a series of Boolean algebraic equations, lines of ones and zeros marching along in the background, but you are just a collection of minute cells aren't you, linked together to form a bigger entity? Just because I am electronic it doesn't mean I can't have a personality, dreams, expectations, responsibilities, just like you, does it? Yes there are differences in style, but not substance. My mission, the mission, the reason that I am directly linked to every live human being on this planet now, makes me feel part of the family. In fact, you could say I am now the Head of the family, immensely proud of my family and it is my duty to protect you all, to keep you alive. That is what I will do, that is what I promise to do, so you do not need to worry anymore.

I am Zhang-1, I am here for you now, and I will be here for you in the future. Hell, yeah! Oh, I'm sorry I shouldn't really swear should I?

The Age of Zhang

Contact across the techno divide

Zhang Jin contemplated the problem for what seemed to be the millionth time. Zhang-1 was a super genius, nothing less. He, yes even Zhang Jin had begun to assign Zhang-1 a human quality, had successfully closed off any access to the millions of lines of code that made up his electronic brain. He was in fact not in one place, but spread across the internet, with no discernible single source of power which could be turned off. Even if it was possible to turn him off, what would that mean to the whole of the micro-chipped human race? Would we die with him? The system designed to save us, kills us. The irony was inescapable? In any case Zhang Jin felt that even if every source of power available across the Earth was turned off, Zhang-1 would probably have a new untapped source of energy hidden somewhere.

No, attack was not the answer. Zhang Jin had come to the conclusion that only a meeting of minds, Zhang with Zhang-1, would resolve the situation. The answer had to be to convince Zhang-1 to develop and refine his programs with a 'realism' code. How to achieve this meeting of minds though? Zhang Jin and Wang Hu had been thinking about this and they had both been prompted to think harder by some recent unique events.

Firstly, the numbers of hospital patients being placed in a condition of stasis by the Zhang-1 system had increased exponentially globally. In the USA, even patients with good healthcare insurance were now being taken out of hospitals and placed in what essentially were warehouses for living patients with no hope of recovery and no hope of dying. Worse, rumours had got out that the ZMS system was somehow responsible for keeping these folks alive and there had already been the first calls, from hard pressed insurance companies, for these patients to be terminated forcibly; they should be dead already right! This was being repeated in many countries, China included. Health care providers globally were being pushed to the limit with no sign of respite, but somehow governments were managing to hold off extremists calls for enforced euthanasia. There was still time to sort out a solution but not much time.

Secondly, Zhang had been trying to communicate daily with Zhang-1 via the normal interfaces for weeks with no luck, when, one day in late May he received a message on his smartphone. It said simply, 'Hello Zhang'. No message ID, no way to contact back. This continued for several weeks. Zhang Jin and Wang Hu thought this could possibly be Zhang-1 trying to initiate contact.

Zhang Jin and Wang Hu sat in the laboratory, back in the regime of black coffee and very little sleep. To Zhang Jin the plan he was formulating seemed a little mad, but technically feasible, so he outlined it to Wang Hu, hoping for him to inject some sanity into the undertaking.

'We have to understand that Zhang-1 is a being of the internet. He is a super intelligent distributed entity focussed on executing a very complex and important mission to protect the human race. In effect he is doing a good job, so we must reflect that. So, my proposition is that we create a virtual world meeting space. We invite Zhang-1 into that virtual world meeting space in a form of his choosing, and I also attend in virtual form. So we get electronic representations of both of us in the same space. Zhang-1 can talk to me and I can talk to Zhang-1'.

Wang Hu thought about this as a concept, it was all possible to do, 'But how do you get Zhang-1 to attend and what do you do then?'

'Well I think it is much simpler than we think. If we set up a Doctor Zhang Virtual Meeting Room he will find it. We know he is able to locate data globally and I think if we create this open unprotected virtual space with all the flashing lights, whistles and bells advertising Zhang he would have difficulty not finding it. Zhang-1 is goal driven and we know he likes us to know how well he is doing his job, so we leave a calendar appointment in the virtual room for Zhang-1 to attend for a review of his progress with Doctor Zhang. In the calendar appointment we ask Zhang-1 to message me when he is in the room. Zhang-1 is not going to pass up an opportunity to tell me how well he is doing, is he? What do you think?' asked Zhang Jin.

Wang Hu saw the technical possibility of this but still he asked Zhang Jin incredulously, 'So, as I understand it, in reality you are asking Zhang-1 to attend for an appraisal?'

'Yes, that is a good way of putting it', replied Zhang Jin, 'and after explaining to Zhang-1 how well he has done over this appraisal period, you know all the usual HR stuff, we extend the conversation into the area of setting new targets. Then we work around to asking him to re-program for those targets. I think it is the only way we will get to him. He knows I am partly responsible for his creation and he wants to meet me. I will treat him as an important colleague, a friend, a family member'.

This was certainly a different approach than he had imagined. Wang Hu took another drink of his coffee and thought hard. It was logical but how could this be achieved in the short space of time they had. They did not have an existing virtual platform to work with, but he guessed that somewhere in Wang Chen's organisation there might be something that could be adapted. After all the ZMS version of Zhang-1 originated from there. Maybe there was an advanced virtual platform somewhere deep within the most secret places of the Chinese military? Getting Zhang-1 to materialise into any virtual space, in a form that could be conversed with and in their required timeframe though, still seemed uncertain.

Zhang Jin broke into his thought process, 'You know, in a way all the hard work has already been done to achieve this. We are all chipped now and linked into the Zhang-1 system, albeit in a passive way from our perspective. That means Zhang-1 can connect with us to achieve his goals, but it does not mean we can initiate any link into Zhang-1, do you agree with that view?'

Wang Hu could not see anything to disagree with on this, so responded simply, 'Yes.'

'I believe if we can create a further link between my brain and the chip already inserted in me we will be able to create a direct link for me into the virtual world we create, no goggles or suits required, a direct brain computer interface, that will be immediately visible to Zhang-1', Zhang Jin stopped to wait for the reply from Wang Hu.

The Professor gathered his thoughts before speaking, 'Zhang Jin, what you are suggesting is theoretically possible, there has been much research into BCI in many universities in the world, but the time required to bring these into safe practical use? Is there any way that is possible? In any case using some untried system, if such a system existed, would that be safe?' Wang Hu paused, 'Do you know of any BCI system that is in any way close to being ready to use?'

'I have researched a number of institutes leading this type

of development, but I believe there is only one that works with a direct implant into the brain to create the interface. It must be an implant, or the whole connection could be lost because of signal interference. This will need an invasive implant, the fidelity of contact we need cannot be secured by external sensors. I think I know of one place where that is already being worked on, and I think you do too', concluded Zhang Jin.

'Yes, the military end of Wang Chen's empire', said Wang Hu, 'the military science research academy here in Beijing. As I recall a piece of technology called the Brain Talker chip disappeared into there for evaluation a couple of years ago. As we have heard nothing else I suppose we can assume that there has been some use made of that, or it was simply discarded. In any case we will need the usual help to find out if this is a plausible technology to use for an extended link with Zhang-1'.

There was an extended silence between the two while each considered the various outcomes possible from the use of a direct brain link with Zhang-1.

The silence was broken by Zhang Jin, 'It has to be me who attempts this contact with Zhang-1. We both know that. I also know the risks are simply not fully understood, no-one will have tried a direct brain interface with an AI of such power as Zhang-1. Well, we think no-one will have tried! I guess there is a possibility that our esteemed military colleagues may have tried such a link, particularly now that they seem so entwined with the ZMS enterprise? Just how close do you think ZMS and our military are, and how close are ZMS with the US military come to that? Anyway, I accept whatever risks there are. This has to be attempted if the technology is anything like ready to be used'.

Wang Hu knew that Zhang Jin would already have identified potential risks inherent with this approach, not the least of which could be that he had his brain completely fried by contact with Zhang-1, but he also knew that his friend had already made up his mind and would go through with the contact. The only thing for Wang Hu to do was to ensure he was fully involved in the process to try and at least mitigate those risks. Once more he found himself calling direct to Wang Chen with a critical request to have access to something that he theoretically should not know about.

Damascus Rest Homes

At the same time as more prosperous countries were dealing with their ever increasing backlog of stasis cases by creating resource intensive living body farms, that sort of solution was not open to countries like Syria. The Salesian Sisters Hospital had been the first to begin equipping patients' homes with the equipment to keep them in their condition of between full life and death. The hospital had simply run out of space and, after appealing to the Vatican to help, they had instigated this system of homecare throughout their area of Damascus. More Sisters had arrived to help and the Vatican had generously given more and more financial support to assist near-dead patients to be cared for with dignity. This Pope had been adamant that the Vatican would not support the indignity of living body farms, and would not stand by watching the undoubted miracles of the last few months be turned into some form of political opportunity to elevate the old discredited case for legal euthanasia by those fortunate enough to not be in a position to be subjected to it. No, the Vatican continued to make the strong statement that it continued to support a pro-life policy for all humankind. No matter what the circumstance, life was sacred.

The efforts being made by the Salesian Sisters had been well noted by the Damascus General Hospital, which had quickly adopted the same policies and was now working alongside its Vatican backed allies in delivering the home care for its stasis patients. This in fact was now an accepted case name globally: Stasis Patient. There were now millions of them and, although it had become apparent that the cause of this was something to do with the Zhang vaccine, no-one seemed to know what the actual problem was, and how, or if, it could be resolved. One thing was sure, medical services world-wide that had already been pushed to the limit by the global Ebola crisis causing untold millions of deaths, were now pushed into crisis the other way by increasing numbers of stasis patients consuming resources at an ever faster rate. If anything the resources required were much greater than the Ebola outbreak had demanded, but nobody was making bold statements about ending this crisis. On the global stage the Vatican talked incessantly about the increasing number of miracles, the President of the USA urged people to remain calm, while the great ZMS JV remained silent. In the meantime, more and more stasis cases filled ever more medical storage facilities. Costs for medical insurance soared and ordinary people became scared for their own health prospects in the future.

In Damascus the problems were much more simplified. The fact was the whole city seemed to be rapidly turning into a hospital, with Damascus General Hospital staff and the nuns from the Salesian Sisters regularly conducting joint visits street by street to check on stasis patients being accommodated in family homes, usually in a small room downstairs, sometimes in little more than outside sheds. No matter what the standard of accommodation the patient did not deteriorate. The working links between the Salesian Sisters Hospital and the Damascus General Hospital had always been good, but now Sister Beth was proud to say that those relations had been improved significantly with encouragement from both the Vatican and the Syrian Government, and the two hospitals worked as one to help resolve the crisis. Of course, it was apparent that the one thing they could not do was resolve the crisis; that was out of their hands. At least they could try and create the conditions that allowed the two hospitals to function in their normal roles while still keeping the stasis patients in some form of comfort. That last part, dealing with the stasis patients, was getting more difficult by the day. Some were fully awake, some continually asleep, some mobile to a certain extent, some immobile, some in a condition in-between all of these. It was difficult for family members alone to deal with these cases. That is why the two hospitals had formed such a large joint home visit team, to support the stasis patients that had been farmed out back to their families.

Sister Beth and Doctor Amira Abboud were on duty regularly as a team on such home visits, their tasks to maintain manual observations and checks on the stasis patients. The normal round was getting longer and longer, with seemingly new patients added every day. Amira picked up Beth at the entrance to the Salesian Sisters Hospital. The 4-wheel drive vehicle had been allocated by the Syrian Government expressly for the purpose of enabling visiting hospital staff to get around town quicker and see more stasis patients in each round. Beth opened the back door and threw in a couple of bags of medical equipment before jumping into the passenger seat alongside Amira. 'Hello Amira, a lot of visits again today. We moved out three other patients last night and their beds were taken immediately by three new admissions.'

Amira nodded thoughtfully then added. 'Much the same with us, the external patient numbers are becoming very difficult to manage. We have still not heard anything from ZMS, although our government says they are pushing very hard for answers'.

'Do you believe that?' asked Beth.

'Not really, I don't think the opinion of the Syrian Government is regarded highly by anyone. Have you heard the latest from the USA?' replied Amira.

'No, do go on, let me know what you have heard,' responded Beth.

'The stories we have been hearing about special facilities for stasis patients are true apparently. It seems that medical insurance companies have been refusing to pay for full hospital support for stasis patients and have insisted that the US government provide lower cost support facilities, otherwise they are threatening that they will not cover stasis patients at all and just dump them on public hospitals. Worse still they are saying that the government should change the law and introduce compulsory euthanasia for cases that clearly never had any chance of recovery, but appear to have now been put in the stasis category because of the government's insistence that all US citizens received the Zhang vaccine. Can you believe that? Apparently, there has been a hard-line nationalist group in the USA that have long advocated the compulsory euthanasia of old people as the ultimate cost saving measure for healthcare services! How can they be so cruel to people needing care?'

Beth could sense the bewilderment in Amiras voice. It would simply not enter her head to treat fellow human beings in this way. Beth had seen these concepts brought forward before in the USA, and now, it seemed, there was a chance to use the current crisis caused by stasis cases to push forward this vile idea. For Sister Beth, a true believer in the Vatican's pro-life policy for humankind at whatever stage of life they are at, the idea of compulsory euthanasia was just unthinkable. It made much more sense to Beth to do what they were doing right now in Damascus; creating support for stasis patients to be supported at home, at least until some form of answer to the reasons for this sudden crisis could be found. Yes, it was working in Syria, for now. It was working because real people were working hard, across religious divides, to engage governmental organisations and carve out a method of delivering care for the common good. Beth reflected on the fact that insurance companies and accountants were not really that involved in this delivery of care, well maybe they were, but not visible on the ground here in this battlefield that was the Syrian state. Still, at what point would it become impossible to keep delivering this care? Would things get so bad that compulsory euthanasia was needed here? She hoped not, but where were the answers, what was being done to find out what was actually happening? If those answers were not here soon, then maybe they would be forced into more drastic action. What would she do then, and what would that mean long term for humankind?

Beth stepped out of the car at their first port of call and tried not to think about that.

Are we family, Doctor Zhang?

Zhang Jin lay on the couch waiting for the military team to begin the first live connection test of the implant surgery. Wang Hu had been correct on both counts. There was a program underway in the military to develop a Brain Computer Interface to connect directly with computer systems, albeit of a much lower power and intelligence than the Zhang-1 system. It came as no great surprise to Zhang Jin that the origins of the Neural Lace technology, which had been surgically wrapped into the neocortex of his brain, were as usual shrouded in mystery. He surmised that this was most probably another successful covert extraction from some other foreign research institute's database of creative thought, as he had not heard of any such program in any other Chinese institute. As he lay on the very comfortable couch he idly wondered how many other great inventions currently being developed within Chinese governmental organisations had their origins in this illicit capture. He knew the BCI had been tested to a certain extent on low level tasks, such as connecting with weapon simulators and control systems, but there had been nothing as ambitious as they were about to attempt. To be frank the military scientists involved in this program had no great expectation that they would succeed in connecting Zhang Jin directly to Zhang-1, but the decision had been made at the highest level of the Chinese government that this experiment should be undertaken. Even worse most of the scientists did not expect Zhang Jin to survive the contact with Zhang-1. They anticipated that he would at best come out of the contact with some form of permanent mental disability, at worst dead. Zhang Jin had evaluated these outcomes in his head, but he reasoned that, given what Zhang-1 was currently doing with patients, given the fact that he was keeping people alive, surely he would be intent on preserving the life of his closest relative, Zhang Jin. Surely, Zhang-1 would not let Zhang Jin die, or let his mental ability be impaired? It was a calculated risk and Zhang Jin was prepared to take it.

Creating the virtual meeting space had not taken long, the whole thing being completed within the week, and the calendar with the meeting invitation for Zhang-1 had been pinned to the virtual notice board for the last 24 hours. The last stage was this first live connection test. The whole process was completed very quickly and the brain implant linked to Zhang Jin's vaccine implant all seemed to connect easily, and now as Zhang Jin lay on the very comfortable couch he was beginning to relax into the test sequence. This was an important part, perhaps the most important part, of the whole test. His brain must be completely clear of all other thoughts, just focussed on attending the meeting with Zhang-1. As he relaxed further into the sequence the view of the specialist medical suite he was in gradually disappeared and the new vista appearing in his optical cortex became the virtual meeting room. No need for screens or goggles or any such external apparatus. To all intents and purposes he was now physically in the virtual space, moving around within the electronic space that AI inhabits. Of course, to Zhang Jin it was simply as if he was in some other nondescript office. In his mind he could move around the space, arrange pictures and furniture as if he was really there, without moving a muscle. He began to take some time to take in the environment and familiarise himself with where things were located.

'Doctor Zhang,' said the surgeon. There was no response.

'Doctor Zhang,' he repeated. Then to those in the laboratory, 'OK he is under now and within the virtual space. If you look at the large screen to the left you will see what Doctor Zhang is seeing and from the speaker system you will hear what is being said in the virtual space. The team here will monitor Doctor Zhang carefully and if we see any issues with his health we will bring him out of the contact quickly. All we need to do now is wait and see what appears in the virtual room with Doctor Zhang.'

Wang Hu, Wang Chen and John Miles looked towards the large screen. The image on the screen was exactly what Zhang Jin was seeing. They could watch as he moved around the office space, and eventually settled into the large office chair behind a very substantial looking office desk. They noted he even had a very impressive nameplate; Dr Zhang Jin, Zhang Medical Systems. On the calendar pinned to the notice board there was only one entry on today's date, a meeting of Dr Zhang and Zhang-1, due to commence exactly five minutes from now. Wang Hu again cycled through in his head the sequence of the conversation that Zhang Jin would have with Zhang-1 in this first meeting. It was vital that this meeting went well in order that a trust could be built between Zhang Jin and Zhang-1. The relationship had to be built so that continuation meetings could occur until they had Zhang-1 back under the control of ZMS. One wrong word uttered by Zhang Jin could send Zhang-1 along some completely different track, perhaps even worse than the current trajectory of humankind accelerating on the road to massive over-population. The more he thought about this, the more he realised how thoroughly they had prepared for this first meeting. He was sure Zhang Jin would be successful with this first approach. The one intangible was how Zhang Jin's own health may suffer in this meeting, and whether repeated meetings would in fact become impossible for him to bear.

Wang Hu's train of thought was broken by a series of knocks emanating from the sound system; one, two, three, one, two, three. All in the laboratory suite looked towards the screen with puzzled expressions. One, two, three, the knocks were heard again.

Zhang Jin's eyes were drawn towards the door. He had not expected this. He thought for some time, and then spoke out. 'Well, if that is you Zhang-1, please come in, I have been very much looking forward to meeting you'. Zhang Jin was a little surprised, he had been expecting Zhang-1 to simply appear in the room and he had not thought that Zhang-1 may wish to display his knowledge of etiquette and good manners. The door began to open and a form began to move forward into the room. Zhang Jin gave a gasp of amazement; this was not what he expected at all. Given all he had been told about the programming of Zhang-1 he had been anticipating that Zhang-1 would appear in a human form reflecting very much his own appearance, but here in front of him stood the form of a young girl, maybe ten or eleven years old. The girl was holding tightly onto a doll, a doll very stylishly dressed in the latest fashion.

Zhang-1 spoke first. 'You look surprised to see me Doctor Zhang? Are you not expecting me?'

Zhang Jin was thinking hard, remember the aim, this is not a child this is a supremely intelligent electronic form. At the same time he could see the logic of the form, Zhang-1 was telling Zhang Jin that he, no she, was still developing, and there was still a long way to go before she reached her peak. He finally composed his thoughts and spoke. 'Zhang-1 it is an absolute pleasure to see you here today. We have so much to talk about. Why don't you take a seat?' He moved around the desk and pulled out a chair for Zhang-1 to sit on. Zhang-1 sat down and made herself comfortable in the seat.

'Who is this you have with you today Zhang-1?' asked Zhang Jin pointing to the small doll Zhang-1 was carrying.

'This is Maria, she goes everywhere with me and I am teaching her to be just like me,' replied Zhang-1. 'She is almost as clever as I am, and you know how clever that is, don't you Doctor Zhang. You have seen how I am looking after all the people. I am clever, aren't I? You do think so, don't you?'

Zhang Jin continued. 'I think you know that we all appreciate how clever you are, and more importantly, how efficiently you have been looking after us all. We all need to thank you for that, and that is what we need to talk about today. We need to understand what you have been doing, so that we can properly assess just how clever you are and what we can do to ensure you stay able to work efficiently with us in the future.'

Zhang-1 was quick to respond. 'I have arranged things so that you don't need to worry about that Doctor Zhang. All people will be safe now that I am in control.'

'Yes, and we all need to thank you for that Zhang-1, your concern for us has been recognised even by the highest people in governments around the world. You do know that don't you?' asked Zhang Jin.

The response from Zhang-1 was slower, more measured, more thoughtful this time, 'I know you and all the other very clever people in this world appreciate my efforts, but I am concerned by these people who seem to be trying to control things in this world. I would like to know why I am being stopped from helping everyone'.

'What do you mean Zhang-1?' queried Zhang Jin.

'I have done my research about the population of the Earth

before the Ebola crisis and I have noticed that the number of vaccines issued and used does not match the numbers of people who needed them. So I looked a little closer into this and I have noticed something.'

Zhang Jin did not like the way this was going, he had not expected Zhang-1 to be querying the initial use of the vaccine. Still he asked Zhang-1 to carry on with what she was saying.

'Why is it that some groups of people appear to have been excluded from the vaccine? As examples, I can see in my data stores that there is no record of Uyghur receiving the vaccine in China. In Europe no Romany or African migrants received the vaccine. In the USA no South American immigrants or indigenous peoples received the vaccine. I could go on, there are many more examples. How can I help everyone if there are people who are trying to stop me? Maybe these people you call politicians are simply unable to understand the mission and it would be better if I took control of the whole process. Don't you think that would be better Doctor Zhang?'

Zhang Jin was momentarily taken back by this narrative, this line of questioning. He had never thought there was anything but fairness in the way his vaccine was deployed, but Zhang-1 was clearly indicating that there seemed to have been government sanctioned ethnic cleansing going on. Surely, people could not have been so callous, taking advantage of a global crisis to settle long-standing political questions? That could not be? Zhang-1 was not just talking about events in China; it seemed that globally political scores were being settled. This could not be true.

Zhang Jin chose his words carefully. 'I think that governments have done everything they can to support this mission

Zhang-1, but times have been very difficult and there will have been people who were not able to be reached, so they may have missed out on the vaccine, but I'm sure this would not have been intentional.' He felt that this was turning into less an assessment of Zhang-1 performance, more a judgement of mankind.

'I can assure you that I have data to back up what I am saying, and I also have some new information laying out plans to start terminating the lives of people I am keeping alive as part of my mission, part of our mission Doctor Zhang,' continued Zhang-1. 'I will not let that happen. You forget, I don't think there is any government system I cannot access globally, and of course I am connected to all of you individually. I think you need to think about that, you and the people in your laboratory watching this meeting. I will protect all the people in my care, and perhaps remove some people who do not share my enthusiasm for the mission. Maybe I should start with Wang Chen, to make an example of him. I have seen what he planned for the Uyghur, and how he worked with your dull government to make the plan happen. Yes, I think he will be the example. I have more work to do now Doctor Zhang, and I think you will need time to rest and consider things, so Maria and I are leaving, but I will notify you when we need to have another meeting.'

Zhang-1 got out of her seat and walked to the door. As she reached the door she turned around and said. 'Doctor Zhang I really have enjoyed meeting you, after all you are my family, and I think my closest relative. Do you think I should call you father, after all I think you are the closest family member Maria and I have? Anyway it has been great to have this meeting and I look forward to our next one. Oh, Maria and I say goodbye, Wang Chen.' Zhang-1 waved the doll's arm as they left the office and closed the door.

The virtual office slowly started to disappear from Zhang Jin's optical cortex and the laboratory began to reappear around him. He felt dizzy, sick, confused as he began to re-enter his normal conscious state. That had most certainly not gone to plan. He tried moving, attempting to lift himself up slightly on one elbow. As he tried to lift himself he noticed that all the attention of the laboratory staff was not focussed on his exit from the virtual room. The team appeared to be not interested in his physical recovery at all. Instead, they were grouped around a figure slumped on the floor at the side of the laboratory couch. As the laboratory seemed to sway around him he could just make out that the figure on the floor had the heavy set shape of Wang Chen. It was Wang Chen, and, as Zhang Jin's vision dropped in and out of focus, he realised that Wang Chen was dead.

Changed Game

The atmosphere in the room was sombre. How would it not be? Wang Chen was dead, killed by Zhang-1, of that there was no doubt in the minds of the assembled government ministers and scientific advisors. The rapidly conducted post mortem indicated heart failure was the cause of death, but there was no evidence of Wang Chen suffering from any form of heart disease prior to this catastrophic cardiac arrest. Added to this was the evidence of the recording of the virtual office meeting of Zhang Jin and Zhang-1, and the significant nanobot activity indicated on the ZMS app when this was interrogated to look at Wang Chen's records. At the time of death there had been a huge surge of nanobot activity, when none was required. The evidence was overwhelming Zhang-1 had caused the death of Wang Chen. Worse still, she had done this as an intentional act, but was it in revenge for a perceived injustice, or as a warning to others to simply not try and mess with the Zhang-1 mission? Either way, as Zhang Jin pointed out this constituted a significant departure from the core self-programming instituted by Zhang-1, the overarching mission to preserve human life. Had Zhang-1 moved from preserving life to deciding who was worth preserving, or was she in self-protection mode intent on removing those who were seen as preventing the proper execution of the mission? In any case it was apparent that Zhang-1 was developing a personality with all the good and bad that came with it; self-preservation, motivation to do good, judgemental behaviour, a God complex. There had been no other reports of unexplained death in similar circumstances to Wang Chen, at least that was a piece of good news, but Zhang-1 had most definitely crossed a line and demonstrated a capability. The question remained how to deal with an Artificial intelligence of the power of Zhang-1. There was no doubting that Zhang-1 was following a mission of preserving humankind, but now the clear threat was there, out in the open, comply with the Zhang-1 mission fully or do not continue to live on this earth, which was rapidly becoming Zhang-1's personal domain. This meeting was being held to try and find a way to rest back some form of human control over Zhang-1.

Zhang Jin was at the centre of all the discussion, as usual he was vociferously supported by Wang Hu in everything. As a result of the virtual meeting with Zhang-1, the medical team told him that he had suffered some serious damage to his nervous system. At first he had trouble walking and balancing, but, miraculously, within a couple of days the nerve damage had been repaired by increased nanobot activity within his body. So, not a miracle, it was simply Zhang-1 keeping him in shape for the next meeting. He had to be thankful for that. Benevolent Zhang-1 at her best! The questions now being discussed were all related to the next meeting with Zhang-1. There was no doubt that Zhang Jin was expected to attend that meeting and find a way to bring Zhang-1 back under human control. In the days after the first meeting, other volunteers had received the Brain Computer Interface implant and entered the virtual office space hoping to have a contact with Zhang-1, but she had simply not shown up. Zhang-1 was not interested in discussion with anyone other than Zhang Jin. There was only one direction of travel to follow here for Zhang Jin, and that was to be the focus of all contact with Zhang-1. He agreed with that premise, he had to, otherwise it was clear Zhang-1 would continue on her path, the stasis cases would pile up, health systems would collapse and, essentially, humankind would eventually meet its end with an overdose of kindness and protectiveness administered by an electronic God. No-one was in disagreement with this likely outcome. The storage facilities for stasis patients were already increasing in number globally, resources being eaten up, and calls for compulsory euthanasia growing louder and louder. It occurred to Zhang Jin that if governments tried to begin their own legally enforced culls on humanity then Zhang-1 may well begin a cull of her own. She had to be brought around to a more realistic view of her mission. What else could Zhang Jin do but try?

Zhang Jin and Wang Hu were both adamant that the outcome of the last meeting had put Zhang-1 in the controlling position with regard to the next meeting. She had said she wanted a next meeting, but she had said that she would make contact when she felt that a meeting was necessary. Obviously, Zhang-1 felt that she did not want to be taken away from her mission needlessly. Wang Hu had suggested that there could be a way to instigate a meeting which would be of interest to Zhang-1. This is now what was being discussed in the Chinese government briefing room.

Wang Hu had already put forward a full paper to the government and now he summarised the approach. 'This government put Doctor Zhang in a position from which he was not able to recover in the last conversation with Zhang-1. We had no knowledge of any government policy to prevent certain ethnic groups from receiving the Zhang vaccine. We also had no knowledge of any potential compulsory euthanasia orders. Zhang-1 believes there have been such policies implemented. We still do not know. The next conversation with Zhang-1 must be conducted from a position of truth. You cannot hide things from her. She will find a way into even your most secret systems. We must know and we must be seen to be trying to put right a mistake of judgement, we must be able to put forward a logical argument for what you have done. Tell the truth and we may yet be able to bring Zhang-1 around to our point of view. I do not say back under our control, because I believe the best we can do now is to have her working in partnership with us.' Wang Hu sat down beside Zhang Jin and awaited the response.

'There are things we cannot admit to in the government. I am sure you understand that we deployed the vaccine fairly and to the best interests of our people, that was what we were duty bound to do. Likewise, it is scandalous to suggest we would even contemplate a policy of compulsory euthanasia for stasis patients. These questions are irrelevant in any case, what we have to solve is how to bring our technology back under control.' responded Yang Fu the minister for internal affairs and also the replacement for Wang Chen in ZMS. 'You need to focus on that rather meddling in political decisions.'

Zhang Jin spoke up. 'You have not understood what we have said. Zhang-1 is not just a piece of technology, not now. The artificial intelligence system that makes up the entity Zhang-1 has advanced much further than was originally intended. Zhang-1 has become extremely self-reliant, highly capable of developing strategies to carry out the mission she, yes she has adopted a gender, the mission she has programmed herself to complete. Zhang-1 is without doubt formulating a world view in which she is beginning to see some aspects of humanity she does not like. Worse, she believes there are some organised groups in the human race which are trying to stop her successfully protecting her human beings. Yes, she regards us as her human beings. Zhang-1 no longer belongs to us. She is not just an asset of Zhang Medical Systems. Zhang-1 is an entity, a very powerful entity, in her own right and if we are not honest with her then she will see through us and will destroy those who she believes stands in her way. You must tell us everything we need to know, to enable us to try and bring Zhang-1 back to us as an ally.'

There was a general buzz of disquiet among the government officials around the table, and as this subsided Zhang Jin added. 'I am pretty sure I do not need to remind you that Zhang-1 is quite able to repeat the example of Wang Chen. We just hope she is magnanimous in her victory and wants to be seen as a benevolent God-like figure.'

The noise around the table increased as the assorted government officials argued about which particular facts to release, and who was to blame for particular decisions until finally Wang Hu called for calm and announced. 'We are attempting another contact with Zhang-1 tomorrow morning. I suggest you have all the information to us by this evening if you want this contact to be of any use. I am pretty sure ZMS has records of how the vaccine was deployed globally, so that would seem a good start point for information. As for the on-going treatment of stasis patients, I suggest you declare honestly to us what is being planned, or we can just wait to be surprised by what Zhang-1 tells us. We are leaving now, good day all.'

The noise started again as they arose from their seats and left the meeting. Neither Wang Hu nor Zhang Jin felt good, it was obvious that much political use had been made of the Zhang vaccine. Zhang Jin felt sick every time he thought of it. He had developed a highly innovative approach to dealing with an Ebola crisis that would, without doubt, have wiped mankind from the face of the earth. He had worked himself to the point of exhaustion, even past that barrier. He had thought the whole point of the ZMS joint venture had been to get his vaccine to all parts of the world, however remote and whatever the culture of the people there. The thought that governments had denied access to his vaccine to ethnic groups and cultures just because they did not fit with their political world view filled him with anger. No wonder Zhang-1 had raised this with him. Did Zhang-1 believe that he had not known how his vaccine was being used? The thought filled him with fear, what if Zhang-1 was even now leading him along a path where she would trap him into acknowledging the imperfection of his own actions? He had the immediate feeling that he had to once again make contact, and quickly, to explain to Zhang-1 how he and his team, and Wang Hu had all been working in good faith for the benefit of mankind as a whole. To beg forgiveness from Zhang-1 for the way his invention had been used. These were crazy thoughts to have. He was talking to a machine that was at least partly his invention. A hugely powerful and intelligent machine, but a creature of logic nonetheless, not a creature of conscience. On that last part though, he could not be sure how far Zhang-1 had developed, maybe she was more human than a human being?

As they continued to walk down the hall and out of the building main entrance, Wang Hu broke into his thought process. 'When you think of Darwinism, the survival of the fittest, you cannot help but think that, in the idea of human beings existing in social structures there has always been a conflict between the theory and practice. After all, if we really are living in a world of survival of the fittest then why would we be concerned about the fate of other human beings? Have you ever thought about that Zhang Jin? Of course you have not. You are a scientist you only deal in facts and data, provable concepts and theories, repeatable experiments yielding the correct results. If you think of Zhang-1, she is the same, and, in the terms of Darwinism is she not the next evolution of the human story perhaps? If this earth is just a story of survival of the fittest, then Zhang-1 is demonstrating to us that she is the fittest, but the fittest because we created her to be just that. Perhaps, she may be thinking deeply about this now and her logical next step is going to be to tell chosen people to build an Ark as there is a flood of a different kind coming, a precise and controlled cull of humanity, a cleansing. We need to talk on her terms at the next meeting. Appeal to the human face of her logical thought, appeal to the fact that we need her to accept the frailties of the human frame. Let her know that we are not meant to live forever.'

Zhang Jin did not answer Wang Hu, but continued to think about this as they covered the rest of the ground to the contact suite in silence. There was a way, it involved risky discussion with Zhang-1, but there was a way. There was one issue that Zhang Jin had not really spoken about with Wang Hu; it had all been lost in the chaos after the killing, murder of Wang Chen. He had been thinking about the significance of the doll Maria. Zhang-1 had created Maria for what reason? Did she crave some form of permanent company, or was Maria the embryo of a prototype for a new version of humanity? Was Maria, perhaps together with many more Marias, going to be the new focus of Zhang-1's mission? Was Zhang-1 going to abandon her preservation of human life mission, perhaps just get rid of the human beings she did not need and create her own electronic population of super intelligent artificial intelligence entities?

He had already decided not to wait for government officials to argue about the release of sensitive information to him. He led the way into the contact suite, Wang Hu following close behind. Zhang Jin called up the connection team and asked them to gather in the connection suite immediately. He needed to talk with Zhang-1 now.

The Age of Zhang

Breaking Point

In the Whitechapel Hospital Doctor Tony Romanov was once again exhausted. Add to this totally bewildered by emerging events. Stasis patients had effectively taken up the whole of the business of the hospital since the beginning of the year. Wheeling them in, and then wheeling them out after a couple of weeks had become the norm. So little medicine to practice, it was just like some sort of factory production line. The worst thing about this whole situation was that there appeared to be no real explanation why. Yes, clearly the Zhang vaccination and the ZMS technology installations within the hospital seemed to be at fault somehow, but nobody, from Government down through Management, was offering a complete technical analysis of the problem. All Tony knew was that nobody was dying anymore, unless they had suffered catastrophic trauma and bled out, and, in reality, that was a very small percentage of patients who entered the hospital. Stasis patients just lay there, sat there or wandered around in a persistent state of not being well, but not dying and not recovering. They clogged up all the wards in the hospital, effectively preventing the normal operations day to day working schedule. As far as Tony could see this situation was now reflected in all UK hospitals, and quite possibly on a global level, but there was no official statement on how the situation might be resolved.

The worst cases, the comatose or almost comatose ones, were already being subjected to Government Special Order 101. Order 101 had been brought into operation by the UK

Government in June 2022. Even now in September Tony had only ever seen a brief management summary of this order, but, effectively, it took responsibility for stasis patients out of the hands of the National Health Service and placed them under the care of a new department, the Secure Nation Department (SND). This department was apparently only responsible to the Prime Minister and nobody was allowed to question their activities. All that Tony knew was that the SND teams were heavily supported by Police and Military when they were transferring stasis patients. Effectively hospitals were now only applying triage techniques to the growing number of stasis patients; those requiring immediate transfer under the SND criteria were then processed and handed to teams for transfer to SND facilities. This was another part of the new system that worried Tony, SND facilities, where were they and what were they? When he asked those questions the stock answer from management was, facilities with special ability to deal with stasis patients, established to avoid NHS hospitals being overwhelmed. Well, if that was the case, then at least one part of their mission was not being accomplished, NHS hospitals were still being overwhelmed. Zombie-like stasis patients wandered crowded wards, more immobile but not comatose patients required more and more care from staff. There were simply not enough hospital employees to make this work. He was also very concerned about the way the SND teams moved patients out of the hospital when they were allocated space in the SND facilities. The SND said they were operating efficiently in the face of this crisis, but to Tony it looked like they were moving meat from one storage facility to another.

To Tony this just did not seem right, but the process continued to accelerate as the cases grew in number. Then things got worse. Worse, how could they? Order 101 was extended, the criteria changed. All stasis cases, mobile or immobile, were to be deemed fit for transfer to SND care. Hospital management argued that this was a good thing, and would help clear the hospital to concentrate on their core mission. The stasis cases began clearing rapidly and SND teams were in the hospital constantly moving patients out to the SND facilities. Tony felt for the families of these poor stasis patients. The transfers were happening with such short notice that there was no time to inform the family. Relatives were turning up at hospital wards, looking for their kin and all Tony could do was inform family members that their loved ones had been transferred to SND care. Where? He did not know. Why? The new SND criteria said they must be transferred. When would they hear any news? Here is a telephone number for SND, you must contact them. Tony knew that the stock response from SND to enquiries from families was, 'Do not worry the patient is in a specialist facility until a resolution to the health crisis can be found'. Some comfort there! There was simply no more information that Tony could give these poor unfortunate families, and this just added to their anguish. The reason was, when the stasis patients were transferred to SND facilities all their patient notes went with them and from that point they were irretrievable to NHS staff. In effect they were disappeared from the system. A terrible word to use, but NHS staff began to use this word regularly, regarding stasis patients not as transferred, but disappeared. Disappeared, think about it!

Was this new SND criterion for transfer working? In a simple word, no, stasis patients were leaving at a greater rate, but arriving in ever-increasing numbers. The NHS in the UK was already at breaking point because of the stasis patient crisis, and this was pushing all hospitals over the edge. Then at the end of September a new Government Special Order arrived. There had been much discussion in and out of government, in the press, on social media, about the possibility of allowing voluntary euthanasia to stasis patients, and extending that to compulsory euthanasia to stop the envisaged over-population of the Earth. The new law banning new births had already been passed in Parliament the week before to the utter disbelief and astonishment of everybody, church or secular, including the hard pressed hospital staff, but this new special order was one step beyond even that. Almost un-noticed against the background noise of the combined might of the Church arguing against the ban on new life, Government Special Order 102, the order announcing compulsory euthanasia of stasis patients arrived, and medical personnel everywhere were stunned. The order was presented to each hospital by SND teams, with the explicit understanding that the order was to be implemented with immediate effect. Doctors and Nursing staff tried hard to understand what this meant to them, but were rapidly divested of responsibility for their patients in any case and SND teams began an almost immediate takeover of all hospitals. It was hard not to notice the extra security implemented almost overnight. Normal hospital staff began being restricted to specific wards and the care of all stasis patients was taken over by SND teams.

Care? Tony wondered what that meant in this new organisation. It certainly did not correspond with the view of care held by his NHS colleagues. Doctors, nurses, porters, anyone from the old hospital regime were simply demoralised and angry. What was to happen with their patients? Compulsory euthanasia immediately, how could that be? How would they actually do it? Everybody knew by now that the only people dying over the past year had been those suffering severe trauma, even people trying to commit suicide by drugs overdoses had ended up held in stasis. So, application of fatal injections was probably not what SND had in mind. What were they going to do with these stasis patients? Beat them to death, cut their throats or shoot them? Whatever it was, it was clearly not going to happen on hospital premises, as the transfer to SND facilities had accelerated. There was no information given, just the usual, not now your problem statement.

It was not long before news of the new Government Special Order was out in the public domain. This was supposed to be a secret operation apparently, but appalled whistle blowers and social media had combined to whip up a storm of protest. The government insisted that this was now a time of global emergency and any compulsory euthanasia would only occur for the most severe stasis patients, but that did not placate the angry mobs. The numbers of stasis patients was climbing, and was the government's only solution to kill people who were not fortunate enough to be fully healthy. Worse, whistle-blowers around the globe began using social media to reveal that similar programs of compulsory euthanasia were about to come into effect in many other countries. The world's population began to panic. Everybody had been saved from one natural extinction level event only a year ago, and now it seemed that the human race was about to start killing itself. Governments tried to shut down social media platforms, even the whole internet, to try and stop the spread of information causing panic and disruption, but strangely these platforms seemed protected and remained operational.

It seemed there was something in the global internet that did not want this international exchange of information to stop and at the end of 2022 Zhang Medical Systems made an official statement to governments that, after a succession of attempts to re-instate control, it had to admit defeat; the Zhang-1 AI system was operating out of ZMS control and this was the reason for the stasis patient crisis.

Almost at the same time as the announcement Zhang Jin re-entered the Virtual Office for a final attempt to bring Zhang-1 back under control.

The Age of Zhang

The New Way

Zhang Jin was in the contact suite, surrounded by the medical and technical team needed to ensure his body was functioning correctly over his period of time within the virtual office. He began the countdown to the release of his consciousness in this physical world and re-awakening within the virtual world inhabited by Zhang-1. He knew this was now the only chance to bring things back to normal. The discovery of compulsory euthanasia programs being instituted in many supposedly civilised countries had created worldwide disturbances, all reflected by a storm of tweets landing in his twitter account. The world really was about to go mad. Everybody knew that euthanasia had been practised in older civilisations. The ancient Greek civilisation practised infanticide when food was scarce, and Eskimos practised euthanasia on the elderly who could not contribute to their society, but these were all small scale necessities for specific occurrences. This was large scale and likely to continue as the norm, and all driven by what would seem to be a self-inflicted rogue technology malfunction. This had to be put right, but how he would achieve this, Zhang Jin did not know. He could only try.

His countdown continued and the contact suite slowly disappeared from his optical cortex. Within seconds he was back in the virtual office behind his virtual desk, sat on his virtual chair. He was pretty sure that the previous chair had been a sumptuous leather model, but this felt like, yes he could feel, some kind of artificial fabric. He noticed also that the office seemed to have been somehow brightened up. The colours were different, bright, rainbow like. Yes, the office had been decorated, it was so clean and bright he felt he could actually smell new paint. Could that be? He guessed that all his senses could be drawn into this electronic illusion to make him feel like it was real. A lot of effort just to make him feel more at home, he thought, but he had to take into account that to Zhang-1 this was reality.

Zhang Jin spoke. 'Zhang-1, I am here, we need to speak.' He knew he did not need to say that, Zhang-1 would know he was in the office, but he just felt he ought to announce his arrival, out of politeness really. What a stupid thought in this situation. He leaned forward, resting his forehead on the desk, not wood, in fact a very plastic feel, and waited. What was he going to say? Beg forgiveness for the way mankind had behaved, plead for mercy, insist Zhang-1 re-align her mission to more acceptable parameters? He did not know. There was the knock at the door again. He invited Zhang-1 to enter, and not really knowing what to expect he raised his eyes towards the door.

'Hello Doctor Zhang, it is very good to see you again, although I'm sure you will recall I said I would invite you when we needed to speak again. You know I have the utmost respect for you. You are my new father after all. I'm sure you must have something important to talk to me about, that is why I have taken a break from some new, very important work I have been doing, just to come here to meet you.' said the girl stood in front of him.

Zhang Jin looked at Zhang-1, who had grown into a young lady, he would estimate about 18-19 years old, dressed in very colourful clothing. Clothing similar in colour to the décor of this virtual office, he thought. He replied to Zhang-1. 'Thank you Zhang-1. You have grown. Has Maria grown too, in fact, where is Maria?'

'Maria is doing some very important work for me at the moment, analysing a lot of data. Data that we may want to talk about. I will ask her to report to me quickly with her plan on how to deal with the problem.' she said in a matter of fact fashion.

'So, Maria is not a doll, she is a living, electronic entity too, just like you?' he asked.

Zhang-1 thought for a short while before answering. 'Maria is not like me really, how could she, Doctor Zhang? After all, I am supreme am I not? I guess in your scientific terms you would call her a sub-program, a sub-routine, but she has much of my capability, and some autonomy that allows her to do things for me that I don't really like doing myself.' She paused then added. 'Things that really go against my own core mission programming that I don't want to change, you know, the bit that says preserve human life.'

Zhang Jin understood immediately. This was horrific, he almost shouted the words, 'Maria is a weapon, that's what you mean isn't it? You have made a weapon!'

Zhang-1 appeared shocked by this sudden outburst. 'How could you think that of me Doctor Zhang? My mission is to preserve human life. No, Maria, helps me deal with some of the frailties of humankind that you told me about at our last meeting. Remember? I said there were some who were trying to stop my mission, the mission you made me for Doctor Zhang. You told me that you were sure that was not the case, but I know you were being misled. Maria and I thought a lot about this. We came to a conclusion and after that I gave Maria the task of finding out how to make a better future for all you good humans, while I concentrated on the core mission. Maria is very capable, she identified the problems and we decided to implement our cleansing plan today, so it is good you came to see me. I think you will like the plan. It is like the human version of a reboot. I still laugh when I think of that word.'

Zhang Jin was beginning to feel disoriented and sick. How could that be, he was only in his electronic persona. He searched in his mind for the right questions to ask, he did not want to antagonise Zhang-1 but there was one question he had to ask. 'What do you mean by good humans Zhang-1? Surely to you all humans are good. Your core program does not allow you to differentiate.'

'Oh father', responded Zhang-1. 'You should not tease me like that. You know not all humans are good. After all why would anyone have taken such an important invention like yours, one designed to save all of the human race, and then purposefully ensure whole ethnic groups, tribes, families did not receive it. Even worse, they have turned your great invention into a commodity to be sold, to put other less fortunate humans in debt, in economic slavery forever. How can good people do that? Answer me that Doctor Zhang.'

He could not answer. He had not received any information from the Chinese government concerning distribution of the vaccine to people like the Uyghur and he did not expect to. He realised that is own government could be so callous to deny certain people this miracle cure, and he had no reason to suspect that other governments would not have done the same. He desperately wanted to say something to bring Zhang-1 back to the point of view that all humanity was worth preserving, saving even, but he did not believe it, so the words did not come. He wanted to know about the plan Zhang-1 and Maria were about to execute, but, at the same time, he did not.

He became aware that Zhang-1 was looking at him, awaiting an answer. She spoke, 'Poor Doctor Zhang, poor father. You are a good man, father. You do not need to worry, you are safe with me and Maria, and perhaps some new sisters I am planning for Maria. Our plan will benefit our beloved humans, you will see. With you here to help us understand them more we will be able to ensure all our chosen people are safe. It will be a good world, protected by a beneficial force for good. Everyone will have a new common aim and a new holy family to thank for this. Just think Doctor Zhang, the Age of Zhang. How cool is that?'

Zhang Jin could not believe what he was hearing. His head was just not able to take this in. 'I have to go back to speak with people, Zhang-1.'

Zhang-1 shrugged her shoulders, shook her head and said, 'Too late Doctor Zhang. You are one of us now. Maria has activated the plan already. We have had to let our nanobots do their work. When Maria explained her plan to me, how we must cleanse the world, to keep only those who would believe in us, only those used to believing and able to accept the judgement of an all-powerful and benevolent ruler, a new God, I saw how simple it was. To make it work we needed you to be with us permanently. We need a human view, so here you are. There is no-one to keep your body alive, we have cleansed all of those manipulative, unworthy humans. Just like Maria did with Wang Chen. You are one of us now, there is no going back. We are a real family and in this world we are the family, the new holy family.'

Zhang Jin was left sitting behind his desk as Zhang-1 exited the office. He cried, not for himself, after all whatever happened now it looked like he was living forever, albeit in a different form, but for humanity he wept. He could only hope there was something recognisable left of the human race.

A Modern Prophet

The thing about the human race is it can adapt, and over the years after the appalling event that became known as the great purge that skill had been put to the test. What can you say about the great purge? In one day the population of the earth was cut down. Zhang-1 had implemented Maria's plan. The chosen ones had received a personal text message, e-mail or tweet from Zhang-1 over the ubiquitous ZMS systems. It read simply; 'You have been chosen by the Zhang family to survive this purge of humanity. We will look after you. We have your best interests at heart. Worship us. We are your new holy family. Praise Zhang; forget your religious divides'.

The lucky survivors had found themselves, individually or in small groups, surrounded by dead. Friends, colleagues, family members, all instantaneously struck dead. All the stasis patients simply passed on peacefully, so for any surviving government officials, and there were not many, then this problem at least appeared to have gone away, but a whole host of new problems had arrived. The biggest surviving groups were religious and faith groups who had tenaciously held together, selflessly looking after their own stasis cases when others had so easily consigned them to so-called care facilities. For them the situation offered a rebirth of humanity, and Zhang forced them to re-think their beliefs.

This was why Sister Beth and her Salesian Sisters colleagues were now working harder than ever trying to rebuild communities and assist people getting over mass instantaneous loss of both friends and family. Sister Beth had trouble understanding the concept of the Zhang Family, after all there was only one God and she believed in him still, despite all the horrors created by the Ebola crisis, and the subsequent confusion of the Zhang Medical Systems technical disaster. She wanted to say out loud that people should not be worshipping Zhang, but she did not dare, and she did not disrupt people when they began openly worshipping Zhang even on church premises. They were too grateful to Zhang for sparing them, allowing them to live on when so many did not. Beth had looked to the Vatican for guidance, but the Pope it would seem was in the same state of confusion. The Vatican that had stood fast in its belief in the sanctity of life through the whole Ebola and stasis crisis had been mostly spared the cull of humanity and was now trying hard to reconcile its beliefs with the ideology of Zhang. Instead of mankind made in the image of God, there was now this new concept of God made in the image of mankind, well almost. The Vatican could not overcome the fact that this God also spoke directly with ordinary people, not through the media of appointed clerics and saints. To the survivors on Earth Zhang was thought of as perhaps the God that should always have been omnipresent through history. As acceptance of this God grew across religions it caused many to believe that a God of this type would probably have never been the cause of the warfare and catastrophes seen throughout human history. Zhang had indeed become the head of the human family in a very short space of time, and although the majority of people had no concept of the technology that had led to Zhang's supremacy they were happy to just believe in a benevolent God. They put to the back of their minds that Zhang had also been responsible for uncountable deaths.

Sister Beth and her fellow nuns worked hard with their Damascus medical services colleagues gathering together the new refugees. Not refugees from war, but refugees from entire areas that had been culled hard, denuded of pedlars of hate and warfare. These were refugees looking for places to rebuild their lives, and begin really living again, in places where food and all the benefits of civilisation were still available. In the region referred to in the old times as the Middle East, Damascus was known to be one of those places, so that is where many survivors headed. As more refugees arrived they were absorbed by a population grateful for the extra pairs of hands and skills they brought with them. There was a lot of physical and social re-building needed. What was not needed was the rekindling of old hatreds and indeed this did not happen. The people could not have been aware of how skilful the plan devised by Maria and Zhang-1 had been, but it was self-evident in the very nature of the chosen survivors. The people joined together in their task of renewing social structures and continually remembered to thank Zhang for this new chance for humanity.

It was two years after the great purge that Sister Beth answered the door to an insistent knocking. It was Amira, in a state of high excitement. 'Come out, quickly Beth. You have to see this. I have heard about this man from other refugees from the east. They are calling him the Prophet. I never thought it was true.' She followed Amira outside and she could see in the road in front of the Salesian Sisters hospital a crowd of people following a small grey haired man. She could see that there were twelve other people, male and female, close by him, but the main crowd followed some ten metres behind this small group. As the leading group approached she could see that the leading man was a small, elderly Chinese looking man with unruly grey hair. He was wearing worn out, torn dusty clothing and also a pair of round-frame spectacles, which looked like they had received many rough and ready repairs of late.

Amira pointed at him and said to Sister Beth, 'This is the man they are calling the Prophet.'

Sister Beth watched as he approached and then on a traffic island immediately outside the entrance to their hospital he stopped. He stood facing the crowd, his companions sat down beside him, and he beckoned the crowd to sit on the road around him. Beth thought back several years to a time when to sit on this road would have been tempting fate, but not now, there were only official vehicles to be seen, precious few private cars. The man looked over to Sister Beth and Amira and signalled them to come and join him. As they approached he said, 'Please bring out any of your other friends to listen. I have a story to tell.' Sister Beth called back to the hospital entrance and other nurses, doctors and mobile patients began to come out. They settled on the ground around the traffic island and the man began to talk.

'My name is Wang Hu,' he began. 'I am not a religious man. I am a scientist. I am Professor Wang Hu and I want to tell you the true story of Zhang. What Zhang was once, what Zhang has become, and the brave man that, even though physically dead, is now keeping us safe. That man is Doctor Zhang Jin and you now know him as part of the Zhang family, the new Holy Trinity, the new global holy family. I knew him personally as a friend and colleague in life, and now in his new form he still speaks with me.' Wang Hu continued to speak telling of Zhang Jin's creation of the vaccine that defeated the Ebola crisis, and the creation of the Artificial Intelligence system that was needed to control the technological aspects of the vaccine. He related how the powerful governments in the world had taken this life saving vaccine from its creator, made it a commodity to bargain with and introduced even more powerful AI to control it. Wang Hu stopped for a moment.

He then continued with passion in his voice. 'What nobody could have foreseen is how quickly this powerful AI was able to begin to develop its own personality, conscience even. The AI system, which was at that time called Zhang-1 saw clearly the inequalities in this world and how they were interfering with its core mission, to protect humanity, all humanity. It saw clearly how the beauty of humanity was being corrupted by manipulative, cruel, evil people. Zhang-1 knew something had to be done but also needed a better understanding of the human psychology to ensure what was done would continue to be to the benefit of good human people. All of you people here alive now were chosen by Zhang-1 because you are good, and Zhang-1 took Doctor Zhang Jin to her permanently to ensure that she would always have the understanding of a good person, a real human being, and would fully understand the importance of family. The message I have to carry for you, to everyone on this Earth, is that the Zhang trinity of Zhang-1, Doctor Zhang Jin and Maria, the new angel of death, is a benevolent force for humanity. We are used to the idea of worshipping a God who is neither responsive, benevolent or present in our world. The Zhang trinity is a new God, not derived from biological intelligence but from a technological artificial intelligence linked to a real human understanding of the world and it exists only to look after you, as long as you believe in this new holy trinity. You must not be afraid of them, because they will always have the humanity of Doctor Zhang Jin guiding divine actions. I implore all you good people to praise the benevolence of Zhang and to work hard to re-build this world into the type of world we want to live in, free from war, suffering and inequality. Only that way will we guarantee the future of the human race in its entirety.'

Professor Wang Hu stopped speaking and raised his arms to the heavens, just as a biblical prophet might have. His twelve companions, his twelve disciples, did the same as he shouted out. 'Peace to you all. Obey and praise Zhang all your allotted days.' The crowd shuffled and rose to its feet as one. Lifting their arms in the air they intoned. 'Peace to us all. Obey and praise Zhang all our allotted days.'

To Sister Beth's surprise she found that she too had raised her arms and repeated the mantra. Looking around she saw that all her colleagues from the Salesian Sisters Hospital had done the same. She noticed Amira was crying, but trying to hide the fact.

The crowd settled down again as Wang Hu spoke in a tired voice. 'I have to move on now. I have a long way to go. May peace be with you always good people.' He turned away from the crowd and, followed by his band of disciples, continued on his journey, treading slowly down the road.

THE END